PENGUIN BOOKS

Fictions

'He more than anyone renovated the language of fiction and thus opened the way to a remarkable generation of Spanish-American novelists. Gabriel García Márquez, Carlos Fuentes, José Donoso, and Mario Vargas Llosa have all acknowledged a debt to him' J. M. Coetzee, *New York Review of Books*

'Borges was the quintessential writer's writer . . . he proved himself to be one of the towering figures of literature in Spanish' James Woodall, *Guardian*

'I love his work because every one of his pieces contains a model of the universe or an attribute of the universe . . . because his stories often take the outer form of some genre from popular literature, a form proved by long usage, which creates almost mythical structures' Italo Calvino

'What Borges offered his readers was a philosophy, an ethical system, a method . . . for the craft of following a revelatory thread through the labyrinth of the universe' Alberto Manguel, *Observer*

'He creates, outside time and space, imaginary and symbolic worlds. It is a sign of his importance that, in placing him, only strange and perfect works can be called to mind' André Maurois

'He is the seer who appears, as if in a dream, to lead the votary forward . . . In one essay he says of Joyce that "he is less a man of letters than a literature". We may without hesitation apply the same description to Borges himself, with the codicil that his is the literature of eternity' Peter Ackroyd, *The Times*

JORGE LUIS BORGES

Fictions

Translated with an Afterword by Andrew Hurley

PENGUIN BOOKS

PENGUIN BOOKS

Published by the Penguin Group
Penguin Books Ltd, 80 Strand, London WC2R 0RL, England
Penguin Putnam Inc., 375 Hudson Street, New York, New York 10014, USA
Penguin Books Australia Ltd, 250 Camberwell Road, Camberwell, Victoria 3124, Australia
Penguin Books Canada Ltd, 10 Alcorn Avenue, Toronto, Ontario, Canada M4V 3B2
Penguin Books India (P) Ltd, 11 Community Centre, Panchsheel Park, New Delhi – 110 017, India
Penguin Books (NZ) Ltd, Cnr Rosedale and Airborne Roads, Albany, Auckland, New Zealand
Penguin Books (South Africa) (Pty) Ltd, 24 Sturdee Avenue, Rosebank 2196, South Africa

Penguin Books Ltd, Registered Offices: 80 Strand, London WC2R 0RL, England

www.penguin.com

These translations first published in *Collected Fictions* in the USA
by Viking Penguin, a member of Penguin Putnam Inc. 1998
First published in Great Britain by Allen Lane The Penguin Press 1999
Published in Penguin Books 2000
Fictions published as a separate volume in Penguin Classics 2000

029

Copyright © Maria Kodama, 1998
Translation and notes copyright © Penguin Putnam Inc., 1998
Afterword copyright © Andrew Hurley, 2000
All rights reserved

This selection was originally published by Emecé Editores, Buenos Aires,
as the collection *Ficciones*
Ficciones is published by arrangement with Grove/Atlantic Inc., New York, New York

The moral right of the translator has been asserted

Set in 11/13.25 pt PostScript Monotype Columbus
Typeset by Rowland Phototypesetting Ltd, Bury St Edmunds, Suffolk
Printed and bound in Great Britain by Clays Ltd, Elcograf S.p.A.

ISBN-13: 978-0-141-18384-8

www.greenpenguin.co.uk

Penguin Books is committed to a sustainable
future for our business, our readers and our planet.
This book is made from Forest Stewardship
Council™ certified paper.

Contents

Fictions*

(1944)

For Esther Zemborain de Torres

The Garden of Forking Paths
(1941)

The Scandal of Father Brown

Foreword

The eight stories* in this book require no great elucidation. The eighth ("The Garden of Forking Paths") is a detective story; its readers will witness the commission and all the preliminaries of a crime whose purpose will not be kept from them but which they will not understand, I think, until the final paragraph. The others are tales of fantasy; one of them—"The Lottery in Babylon"—is not wholly innocent of symbolism. I am not the first author of the story called "The Library of Babel"; those curious as to its history and prehistory may consult the appropriate page of *Sur,* * No. 59, which records the heterogeneous names of Leucippus and Lasswitz, Lewis Carroll and Aristotle. In "The Circular Ruins," all is unreal; in "Pierre Menard, Author of the *Quixote*," the unreality lies in the fate the story's protagonist imposes upon himself. The catalog of writings I have ascribed to him is not terribly amusing, but it is not arbitrary, either; it is a diagram of his mental history. . . .

It is a laborious madness and an impoverishing one, the madness of composing vast books—setting out in five hundred pages an idea that can be perfectly related orally in five minutes. The better way to go about it is to pretend that those books already exist, and offer a summary, a commentary on them. That was Carlyle's procedure in *Sartor Resartus*, Butler's in *The Fair Haven*— though those works suffer under the imperfection that they themselves are books, and not a whit less tautological than the others. A more reasonable, more inept, and more lazy man, I have

5

chosen to write notes on *imaginary* books. Those notes are "Tlön, Uqbar, Orbis Tertius" and "A Survey of the Works of Herbert Quain."

J.L.B

Tlön, Uqbar, Orbis Tertius

I

I owe the discovery of Uqbar to the conjunction of a mirror and an encyclopedia. The mirror troubled the far end of a hallway in a large country house on Calle Gaona, in Ramos Mejía*; the encyclopedia is misleadingly titled *The Anglo-American Cyclopaedia* (New York, 1917), and is a literal (though also laggardly) reprint of the 1902 *Encyclopædia Britannica*. The event took place about five years ago.

Bioy Casares* had come to dinner at my house that evening, and we had lost all track of time in a vast debate over the way one might go about composing a first-person novel whose narrator would omit or distort things and engage in all sorts of contradictions, so that a few of the book's readers—a *very* few— might divine the horrifying or banal truth. Down at that far end of the hallway, the mirror hovered, shadowing us. We discovered (very late at night such a discovery is inevitable) that there is something monstrous about mirrors. That was when Bioy remembered a saying by one of the heresiarchs of Uqbar: *Mirrors and copulation are abominable, for they multiply the number of mankind.* I asked him where he'd come across that memorable epigram, and he told me it was recorded in *The Anglo-American Cyclopaedia*, in its article on Uqbar.

The big old house (we had taken it furnished) possessed a copy of that work. On the last pages of Volume XLVI we found an article on Uppsala; on the first of Volume XLVII, "Ural-Altaic Languages"—not a word on Uqbar. Bioy, somewhat bewildered, consulted the volumes of the Index. He tried every possible spelling: Ukbar, Ucbar, Ookbar, Oukbahr . . . all in vain. Before he left, he told me it was a region in Iraq or Asia Minor. I confess I nodded a bit uncomfortably; I surmised that that undocumented country and its anonymous heresiarch were a fiction that Bioy had invented on the spur of the moment, out of modesty, in order to justify a fine-sounding epigram. A sterile search through one of the atlases of Justus Perthes reinforced my doubt.

The next day, Bioy called me from Buenos Aires. He told me he had the article on Uqbar right in front of him—in Volume XLVI* of the encyclopedia. The heresiarch's name wasn't given, but the entry did report his doctrine, formulated in words almost identical to those Bioy had quoted, though from a literary point of view perhaps inferior. Bioy had remembered its being "copulation and mirrors are abominable," while the text of the encyclopedia ran *For one of those gnostics, the visible universe was an illusion or, more precisely, a sophism. Mirrors and fatherhood are hateful because they multiply and proclaim it.* I told Bioy, quite truthfully, that I'd like to see that article. A few days later he brought it to me—which surprised me, because the scrupulous cartographic indices of Ritter's *Erdkunde* evinced complete and total ignorance of the existence of the name Uqbar.

The volume Bioy brought was indeed Volume XLVI of the *Anglo-American Cyclopaedia.* On both the false cover and spine, the alphabetical key to the volume's contents (Tor-Upps) was the same as ours, but instead of 917 pages, Bioy's volume had 921. Those four additional pages held the article on Uqbar—an article not contemplated (as the reader will have noted) by the alphabetical key. We later compared the two volumes and found that there was no further difference between them. Both (as I believe I have said) are reprints of the tenth edition of the *Encyclopædia Britannica.* Bioy had purchased his copy at one of his many sales.

We read the article with some care. The passage that Bioy had recalled was perhaps the only one that might raise a reader's eyebrow; the rest seemed quite plausible, very much in keeping with the general tone of the work, even (naturally) somewhat boring. Rereading it, however, we discovered that the rigorous writing was underlain by a basic vagueness. Of the fourteen names that figured in the section on geography, we recognized only three (Khorasan, Armenia, Erzerum), all interpolated into the text ambiguously. Of the historical names, we recognized only one: the impostor-wizard Smerdis, and he was invoked, really, as a metaphor. The article seemed to define the borders of Uqbar, but its nebulous points of reference were rivers and craters and mountain chains of the region itself. We read, for example, that the Axa delta and the lowlands of Tsai Khaldun mark the southern boundary, and that wild horses breed on the islands of the delta. That was at the top of page 918. In the section on Uqbar's history (p. 920), we learned that religious persecutions in the thirteenth century had forced the orthodox to seek refuge on those same islands, where their obelisks are still standing and their stone mirrors are occasionally unearthed. The section titled "Language and Literature" was brief. One memorable feature: the article said that the literature of Uqbar was a literature of fantasy, and that its epics and legends never referred to reality but rather to the two imaginary realms of Mle'khnas and Tlön. . . . The bibliography listed four volumes we have yet to find, though the third—Silas Haslam's *History of the Land Called Uqbar* (1874)—does figure in the catalogs published by Bernard Quaritch, Bookseller.[1] The first, *Lesbare und lesenswerthe Bemerkungen über das Land Ukkbar in Klein-Asien*, published in 1641, is the work of one Johannes Valentinus Andreä. That fact is significant: two or three years afterward, I came upon that name in the unexpected pages of De Quincey (*Writings*, Vol. XIII*), where I learned that it belonged

1. Haslam was also the author of *A General History of Labyrinths*.

9

to a German theologian who in the early seventeenth century described an imaginary community, the Rosy Cross—which other men later founded, in imitation of his foredescription.

That night, Bioy and I paid a visit to the National Library, where we pored in vain through atlases, catalogs, the yearly indices published by geographical societies, the memoirs of travelers and historians—no one had ever been in Uqbar. Nor did the general index in Bioy's copy of the encyclopedia contain that name. The next day, Carlos Mastronardi* (whom I had told about all this) spotted the black-and-gold spines of the *Anglo-American Cyclopaedia* in a bookshop at the corner of Corrientes and Talcahuano. . . .He went in and consulted Volume XLVI. Naturally, he found not the slightest mention of Uqbar.

II

Some limited and waning memory of Herbert Ashe, an engineer for the Southern Railway Line, still lingers in the hotel at Adrogué, among the effusive honeysuckle vines and in the illusory depths of the mirrors. In life, Ashe was afflicted with unreality, as so many Englishmen are; in death, he is not even the ghost he was in life. He was tall and phlegmatic and his weary rectangular beard had once been red. I understand that he was a widower, and without issue. Every few years he would go back to England, to make his visit (I am judging from some photographs he showed us) to a sundial and a stand of oak trees. My father had forged one of those close English friendships with him (the first adjective is perhaps excessive) that begin by excluding confidences and soon eliminate conversation. They would exchange books and newspapers; they would wage taciturn battle at chess. . . .I recall Ashe on the hotel veranda, holding a book of mathematics, looking up sometimes at the irrecoverable colors of the sky. One evening, we spoke about the duodecimal number system, in which twelve is written 10. Ashe said that by coincidence he was just then transposing some duodecimal table or other to sexagesimal (in which sixty is written 10). He added that he'd been commissioned to perform that task by a Norwegian man . . . in Rio Grande do Sul. Ashe and I had known each other for eight years, and he had never mentioned a stay in Brazil. We spoke of the bucolic rural life, of *capangas*,* of the Brazilian etymology of the word "*gaucho*" (which some older folk in Uruguay still pronounce as *ga-úcho*), and nothing more was said—God forgive me—of duodecimals. In September of 1937 (my family and I were no longer at the hotel), Herbert Ashe died of a ruptured aneurysm. A few days before his death, he had received a sealed, certified package from Brazil containing a book printed in octavo major. Ashe left it in the bar, where, months later, I found it. I began to leaf through it and suddenly I experienced a slight, astonished sense of dizziness that I shall not describe, since this is the story not of my emotions but of Uqbar and Tlön and Orbis Tertius. (On one particular Islamic night, which is called the Night of Nights, the secret portals of the heavens open wide and the water in the water jars is sweeter than on other nights; if those gates had opened as I sat there, I would not have felt what I was feeling that evening.) The book was written in English, and it consisted of 1001 pages. On the leather-bound volume's yellow spine I read these curious words, which were repeated on the false cover: *A First Encyclopædia* of Tlön. Vol. XI. Hlaer to Jangr. There was no date or place of publication. On the first page and again on the onionskin page that covered one of the color illustrations there was stamped a blue oval with this inscription: *Orbis Tertius*. Two years earlier, I had discovered in one of the volumes of a certain pirated encyclopedia a brief description of a false country; now fate had set before me something much more precious and painstaking. I now held in my hands a vast and systematic fragment of the entire history of an unknown planet, with its architectures and its playing cards, the horror of its mythologies and the murmur of its tongues, its emperors and its seas, its minerals and its birds and fishes, its algebra and its fire, its theological and metaphysical controversies—all joined, articulated, coherent, and with no visible doctrinal purpose or hint of parody.

In the "Volume Eleven" of which I speak, there are allusions to later and earlier volumes. Néstor Ibarra,* in a now-classic article in the *N.R.F.*, denied that such companion volumes exist; Ezequiel Martínez Estrada* and Drieu La Rochelle* have rebutted that doubt, perhaps victoriously. The fact is, the most diligent searches have so far proven futile. In vain have we ransacked the libraries of the two Americas and Europe. Alfonso Reyes*, weary of those "subordinate drudgeries of a detective nature," has proposed that between us, we undertake to *reconstruct* the many massive volumes that are missing: *ex ungue leonem.* He figures, half-seriously, half in jest, that a generation of Tlönists would suffice. That bold estimate takes us back to the initial problem: Who, singular or plural, invented Tlön? The plural is, I suppose, inevitable, since the hypothesis of a single inventor—some infinite Leibniz working in obscurity and self-effacement—has been unanimously discarded. It is conjectured that this "brave new world" is the work of a secret society of astronomers, biologists, engineers, metaphysicians, poets, chemists, algebrists, moralists, painters, geometers, . . . , guided and directed by some shadowy man of genius. There are many men adept in those diverse disciplines, but few capable of imagination—fewer still capable of subordinating imagination to a rigorous and systematic plan. The plan is so vast that the contribution of each writer is infinitesimal.

At first it was thought that Tlön was a mere chaos, an irresponsible act of imaginative license; today we know that it is a cosmos, and that the innermost laws that govern it have been formulated, however provisionally so. Let it suffice to remind the reader that the apparent contradictions of Volume Eleven are the foundation stone of the proof that the other volumes do in fact exist: the order that has been observed in it is just that lucid, just that fitting.

Popular magazines have trumpeted, with pardonable excess, the zoology and topography of Tlön. In my view, its transparent tigers and towers of blood do not perhaps merit the constant attention of *all* mankind, but I might be so bold as to beg a few moments to outline its conception of the universe.

Hume declared for all time that while Berkeley's arguments admit not the slightest refutation, they inspire not the slightest conviction. That pronouncement is entirely true with respect to the earth, entirely false with respect to Tlön. The nations of that planet are, congenitally, idealistic. Their language and those things derived from their language—religion, literature, metaphysics—presuppose idealism. For the people of Tlön, the world is not an amalgam of *objects* in space; it is a heterogeneous series of independent *acts*—the world is successive, temporal, but not spatial. There are no nouns in the conjectural *Ursprache* of Tlön, from which its "present-day" languages and dialects derive: there are impersonal verbs, modified by monosyllabic suffixes (or prefixes) functioning as adverbs. For example, there is no noun that corresponds to our word "moon," but there is a verb which in English would be "to moonate" or "to enmoon." "The moon rose above the river" is "*hlör u fang axaxaxas mlö*," or, as Xul Solar* succinctly translates: *Upward, behind the onstreaming it mooned.*

That principle applies to the languages of the southern hemisphere. In the northern hemisphere (about whose *Ursprache* Volume Eleven contains very little information), the primary unit is not the verb but the monosyllabic adjective. Nouns are formed by stringing together adjectives. One does not say "moon"; one says "aerial-bright above dark-round" or "soft-amberish-celestial" or any other string. In this case, the complex of adjectives corresponds to a real object, but that is purely fortuitous. The literature of the northern hemisphere (as in Meinong's subsisting world) is filled with ideal objects, called forth and dissolved in an instant, as the poetry requires. Sometimes mere simultaneity

13

creates them. There are things composed of two terms, one visual and the other auditory: the color of the rising sun and the distant caw of a bird. There are things composed of many: the sun and water against the swimmer's breast, the vague shimmering pink one sees when one's eyes are closed, the sensation of being swept along by a river and also by Morpheus. These objects of the second degree may be combined with others; the process, using certain abbreviations, is virtually infinite. There are famous poems composed of a single enormous word; this word is a "poetic object" created by the poet. The fact that no one believes in the reality expressed by these nouns means, paradoxically, that there is no limit to their number. The languages of Tlön's northern hemisphere possess all the nouns of the Indo-European languages—and many, many more.

It is no exaggeration to say that the classical culture of Tlön is composed of a single discipline—psychology—to which all others are subordinate. I have said that the people of that planet conceive the universe as a series of mental processes that occur not in space but rather successively, in time. Spinoza endows his inexhaustible deity with the attributes of spatial extension and of thought; no one in Tlön would understand the juxtaposition of the first, which is typical only of certain states, and the second—which is a perfect synonym for the cosmos. Or to put it another way: space is not conceived as having duration in time. The perception of a cloud of smoke on the horizon and then the countryside on fire and then the half-extinguished cigarette that produced the scorched earth is considered an example of the association of ideas.

This thoroughgoing monism, or idealism, renders science null. To explain (or pass judgment on) an event is to link it to another; on Tlön, that joining-together is a posterior state of the *subject*, and can neither affect nor illuminate the prior state. Every mental state is irreducible: the simple act of giving it a name—i.e., of classifying it—introduces a distortion, a "slant" or "bias." One might well deduce, therefore, that on Tlön there are no sciences— or even any "systems of thought." The paradoxical truth is that systems of thought do exist, almost countless numbers of them. Philosophies are much like the nouns of the northern hemisphere; the fact that every philosophy is by definition a dialectical game, a *Philosophie des Als Ob*, has allowed them to proliferate. There are systems upon systems that are incredible but possessed of a pleasing architecture or a certain agreeable sensationalism. The metaphysicians of Tlön seek not truth, or even plausibility—they seek to amaze, astound. In their view, metaphysics is a branch of the literature of fantasy. They know that a system is naught but the subordination of all the aspects of the universe to one of those aspects—*any* one of them. Even the phrase "all the aspects" should be avoided, because it implies the impossible addition of the present instant and all those instants that went before. Nor is the plural "those instants that went before" legitimate, for it implies another impossible operation. . . .One of the schools of philosophy on Tlön goes so far as to deny the existence of time; it argues that the present is undefined and indefinite, the future has no reality except as present hope, and the past has no reality except as present recollection.[1] Another school posits that all time has already passed, so that our life is but the crepuscular memory, or crepuscular reflection, doubtlessly distorted and mutilated, of an irrecoverable process. Yet another claims that the history of the universe—and in it, our lives and every faintest detail of our lives—is the handwriting of a subordinate god trying to communicate with a demon. Another, that the universe might be compared to those cryptograms in which not all the symbols count, and only what happens every three hundred nights is actually real. Another, that while we sleep here, we are awake somewhere else, so that every man is in fact two men.

1. Russell (*The Analysis of Mind* [1921], p. 159) posits that the world was created only moments ago, filled with human beings who "remember" an illusory past.

Of all the doctrines of Tlön, none has caused more uproar than materialism. Some thinkers have formulated this philosophy (generally with less clarity than zeal) as though putting forth a paradox. In order to make this inconceivable thesis more easily understood, an eleventh-century heresiarch[1] conceived the sophism of the nine copper coins, a paradox as scandalously famous on Tlön as the Eleatic aporiae to ourselves. There are many versions of that "specious argument," with varying numbers of coins and discoveries; the following is the most common:

On Tuesday, X is walking along a deserted road and loses nine copper coins. On Thursday, Y finds four coins in the road, their luster somewhat dimmed by Wednesday's rain. On Friday, Z discovers three coins in the road. Friday morning X finds two coins on the veranda of his house.

From this story the heresiarch wished to deduce the reality—i.e., the continuity in time—of those nine recovered coins. "It is absurd," he said, "to imagine that four of the coins did not exist from Tuesday to Thursday, three from Tuesday to Friday afternoon, two from Tuesday to Friday morning. It is logical to think that they in fact *did* exist—albeit in some secret way that we are forbidden to understand—at every moment of those three periods of time."

The language of Tlön resisted formulating this paradox; most people did not understand it. The "common sense" school at first simply denied the anecdote's veracity. They claimed it was a verbal fallacy based on the reckless employment of two neologisms, words unauthorized by standard usage and foreign to all rigorous thought: the two verbs "find" and "lose," which, since they presuppose the identity of the nine first coins and the nine

1. A "century," in keeping with the duodecimal system in use on Tlön, is a period of 144 years.

latter ones, entail a *petitio principii*. These critics reminded their listeners that all nouns *(man, coin, Thursday, Wednesday, rain)* have only metaphoric value. They denounced the misleading detail that "[the coins'] luster [was] somewhat dimmed by Wednesday's rain" as presupposing what it attempted to prove: the continuing existence of the four coins from Tuesday to Thursday. They explained that "equality" is one thing and "identity" another, and they formulated a sort of *reductio ad absurdum*—the hypothetical case of nine men who on nine successive nights experience a sharp pain. Would it not be absurd, they asked, to pretend that the men had suffered one and the same pain?[1] They claimed that the heresiarch was motivated by the blasphemous desire to attribute the divine category *Being* to a handful of mere coins, and that he sometimes denied plurality and sometimes did not. They argued: If equality entailed identity, one would have to admit that the nine coins were a single coin.

Incredibly, those refutations did not put an end to the matter. A hundred years after the problem had first been posed, a thinker no less brilliant than the heresiarch, but of the orthodox tradition, formulated a most daring hypothesis. His happy conjecture was that there is but a single subject; that indivisible subject is every being in the universe, and the beings of the universe are the organs and masks of the deity. X is Y and is *also* Z. Z discovers three coins, then, because he remembers that X lost them; X finds two coins on the veranda of his house because he remembers that the others have been found. . . . Volume Eleven suggests that this idealistic pantheism triumphed over all other schools of thought for three primary reasons: first, because it repudiated solipsism; second, because it left intact the psychological foundation of the

1. Today, one of Tlön's religions contends, platonically, that a certain pain, a certain greenish-yellow color, a certain temperature, and a certain sound are all the same, single reality. All men, in the dizzying instant of copulation, are the same man. All men who speak a line of Shakespeare *are* William Shakespeare.

sciences; and third, because it preserved the possibility of religion. Schopenhauer (passionate yet lucid Schopenhauer) formulates a very similar doctrine in the first volume of his *Parerga und Paralipomena*.

Tlön's geometry is made up of two rather distinct disciplines—visual geometry and tactile geometry. Tactile geometry corresponds to our own, and is subordinate to the visual. Visual geometry is based on the surface, not the point; it has no parallel lines, and it claims that as one's body moves through space, it modifies the shapes that surround it. The basis of Tlön's arithmetic is the notion of indefinite numbers; it stresses the importance of the concepts "greater than" and "less than," which our own mathematicians represent with the symbols $>$ and $<$. The people of Tlön are taught that the act of counting modifies the amount counted, turning indefinites into definites. The fact that several persons counting the same quantity come to the same result is for the psychologists of Tlön an example of the association of ideas or of memorization.—We must always remember that on Tlön, the subject of knowledge is one and eternal.

Within the sphere of literature, too, the idea of the single subject is all-powerful. Books are rarely signed, nor does the concept of plagiarism exist: It has been decided that all books are the work of a single author who is timeless and anonymous. Literary criticism often invents authors: It will take two dissimilar works—the *Tao Te Ching* and the *1001 Nights*, for instance—attribute them to a single author, and then in all good conscience determine the psychology of that most interesting *homme de lettres*. . . .

Their books are also different from our own. Their fiction has but a single plot, with every imaginable permutation. Their works of a philosophical nature invariably contain both the thesis and the antithesis, the rigorous *pro* and *contra* of every argument. A book that does not contain its counterbook is considered incomplete.

Century upon century of idealism could hardly have failed to influence reality. In the most ancient regions of Tlön one may, not infrequently, observe the duplication of lost objects: Two persons are looking for a pencil; the first person finds it, but says nothing; the second finds a second pencil, no less real, but more in keeping with his expectations. These secondary objects are called *hrönir*, and they are, though awkwardly so, slightly longer. Until recently, *hrönir* were the coincidental offspring of distraction and forgetfulness. It is hard to believe that they have been systematically produced for only about a hundred years, but that is what Volume Eleven tells us. The first attempts were unsuccessful, but the *modus operandi* is worth recalling: The warden of one of the state prisons informed his prisoners that there were certain tombs in the ancient bed of a nearby river, and he promised that anyone who brought in an important find would be set free. For months before the excavation, the inmates were shown photographs of what they were going to discover. That first attempt proved that hope and greed can be inhibiting; after a week's work with pick and shovel, the only *hrön* unearthed was a rusty wheel, dated some time *later* than the date of the experiment. The experiment was kept secret, but was repeated afterward at four high schools. In three of them, the failure was virtually complete; in the fourth (where the principal happened to die during the early excavations), the students unearthed—or produced—a gold mask, an archaic sword, two or three clay amphorae, and the verdigris'd and mutilated torso of a king with an inscription on the chest that has yet to be deciphered. Thus it was discovered that no witnesses who were aware of the experimental nature of the search could be allowed near the site. . . . Group research projects produce conflicting finds; now individual, virtually spur-of-the-moment projects are preferred. The systematic production of *hrönir* (says Volume Eleven) has been of invaluable aid to archaeologists, making it possible not only to interrogate but even to modify the past, which is now no less plastic, no less malleable than the future. A curious bit of information: *hrönir* of the second and third remove—*hrönir* derived from another *hrön*, and *hrönir* derived from the *hrön* of a *hrön*—exaggerate the aberrations of the first; those of the fifth remove are almost identical; those of the ninth can be confused with those of the second; and those of the eleventh remove exhibit a purity of line that even the originals do not exhibit. The process is periodic: The *hrönir* of the twelfth remove begin to degenerate. Sometimes stranger and purer than any *hrön* is the *ur*—the thing produced by suggestion, the object brought forth by hope. The magnificent gold mask I mentioned is a distinguished example.

Things duplicate themselves on Tlön; they also tend to grow vague or "sketchy," and to lose detail when they begin to be forgotten. The classic example is the doorway that continued to exist so long as a certain beggar frequented it, but which was lost to sight when he died. Sometimes a few birds, a horse, have saved the ruins of an amphitheater.

Salto Oriental, 1940

Postscript—1947

I reproduce the article above exactly as it appeared in the *Anthology of Fantastic Literature* (1940), the only changes being editorial cuts of one or another metaphor and a tongue-in-cheek sort of summary that would now be considered flippant. So many things have happened since 1940. . . .Allow me to recall some of them:

In March of 1941, a handwritten letter from Gunnar Erfjord was discovered in a book by Hinton that had belonged to Herbert Ashe. The envelope was postmarked Ouro Preto; the mystery of Tlön was fully elucidated by the letter. It confirmed Martínez Estrada's hypothesis: The splendid story had begun sometime in the early seventeenth century, one night in Lucerne or London. A secret benevolent society (which numbered among its members

Dalgarno and, later, George Berkeley) was born; its mission: to invent a country. In its vague initial program, there figured "hermetic studies," philanthropy, and the Kabbalah. (The curious book by Valentinus Andreä dates from that early period.) After several years of confabulations and premature collaborative drafts, the members of the society realized that one generation would not suffice for creating and giving full expression to a country. They decided that each of the masters that belonged to the society would select a disciple to carry on the work. That hereditary arrangement was followed; after an interim of two hundred years, the persecuted fraternity turned up again in the New World. In 1824, in Memphis, Tennessee, one of the members had a conversation with the reclusive millionaire Ezra Buckley. Buckley, somewhat contemptuously, let the man talk—and then laughed at the modesty of the project. He told the man that in America it was nonsense to invent a country—what they ought to do was invent a planet. To that giant of an idea he added another, the brainchild of his nihilism[1]: The enormous enterprise must be kept secret. At that time the twenty volumes of the *Encyclopædia Britannica* were all the rage; Buckley suggested a systematic encyclopedia of the illusory planet. He would bequeath to them his gold-veined mountains, his navigable rivers, his prairies thundering with bulls and buffalo, his Negroes, his brothels, and his dollars, he said, under one condition: "The work shall make no pact with the impostor Jesus Christ." Buckley did not believe in God, yet he wanted to prove to the nonexistent God that mortals could conceive and shape a world. Buckley was poisoned in Baton Rouge in 1828; in 1914 the society sent its members (now numbering three hundred) the final volume of the *First Encyclopædia of Tlön*. It was published secretly: the forty volumes that made up the work (the grandest work of letters ever undertaken by humankind) were to be the basis for another, yet more

1. Buckley was a freethinker, a fatalist, and a defender of slavery.

painstaking work, to be written this time not in English but in one of the languages of Tlön. That survey of an illusory world was tentatively titled *Orbis Tertius*, and one of its modest demiurges was Herbert Ashe—whether as agent or colleague of Gunnar Erfjord, I cannot say. His receipt of a copy of Volume Eleven seems to favor the second possibility. But what about the others? In 1942, the plot thickened. I recall with singular clarity one of the first events that occurred, something of whose premonitory nature I believe I sensed even then. It took place in an apartment on Laprida, across the street from a high, bright balcony that faced the setting sun. Princess Faucigny Lucinge had received from Poitiers a crate containing her silver table service. From the vast innards of a packing case emblazoned with international customs stamps she removed, one by one, the fine unmoving things: plate from Utrecht and Paris chased with hard heraldic fauna, . . . , a samovar. Among the pieces, trembling softly but perceptibly, like a sleeping bird, there throbbed, mysteriously, a compass. The princess did not recognize it. Its blue needle yearned toward magnetic north; its metal casing was concave; the letters on its dial belonged to one of the alphabets of Tlön. That was the first intrusion of the fantastic world of Tlön into the real world.

An unsettling coincidence made me a witness to the second intrusion as well. This event took place some months later, in a sort of a country general-store-and-bar owned by a Brazilian man in the Cuchilla Negra. Amorim* and I were returning from Sant'Anna. There was a freshet on the Tacuarembó; as there was no way to cross, we were forced to try (to try to endure, that is) the rudimentary hospitality at hand. The storekeeper set up some creaking cots for us in a large storeroom clumsy with barrels and stacks of leather. We lay down, but we were kept awake until almost dawn by the drunkenness of an unseen neighbor, who swung between indecipherable streams of abuse and loudly sung snatches of *milongas*—or snatches of the same *milonga*, actually.

As one can imagine, we attributed the man's insistent carrying-on to the storekeeper's fiery rotgut. . . .By shortly after daybreak, the man was dead in the hallway. The hoarseness of his voice had misled us—he was a young man. In his delirium, several coins had slipped from his wide gaucho belt, as had a gleaming metal cone about a die's width in diameter. A little boy tried to pick the cone-shaped object up, but in vain; a full-grown man could hardly do it. I held it for a few minutes in the palm of my hand; I recall that its weight was unbearable, and that even after someone took it from me, the sensation of terrible heaviness endured. I also recall the neat circle it engraved in my flesh. That evidence of a very small yet extremely heavy object left an unpleasant aftertaste of fear and revulsion. A *paisano* suggested that we throw it in the swollen river. Amorim purchased it for a few pesos. No one knew anything about the dead man, except that "he came from the border." Those small, incredibly heavy cones (made of a metal not of this world) are an image of the deity in certain Tlönian religions.

Here I end the personal portion of my narration. The rest lies in every reader's memory (if not his hope or fear). Let it suffice to recall, or mention, the subsequent events, with a simple brevity of words which the general public's concave memory will enrich or expand:

In 1944, an investigator from *The Nashville American* unearthed the forty volumes of *The First Encyclopædia of Tlön* in a Memphis library. To this day there is some disagreement as to whether that discovery was accidental or consented to and guided by the directors of the still-nebulous *Orbis Tertius*; the second supposition is entirely plausible. Some of the unbelievable features of Volume Eleven (the multiplication of *hrönir*, for example) have been eliminated or muted in the Memphis copy. It seems reasonable to suppose that the cuts obey the intent to set forth a world that is not *too* incompatible with the real world. The spread of Tlönian objects through various countries would complement that plan. . . .[1] At any rate, the international press made a great hue and cry about this "find." Handbooks, anthologies, surveys, "literal translations," authorized and pirated reprints of Mankind's Greatest Masterpiece filled the world, and still do. Almost immediately, reality "caved in" at more than one point. The truth is, it wanted to cave in. Ten years ago, any symmetry, any system with an appearance of order—dialectical materialism, anti-Semitism, Nazism—could spellbind and hypnotize mankind. How could the world not fall under the sway of Tlön, how could it not yield to the vast and minutely detailed evidence of an ordered planet? It would be futile to reply that reality is also orderly. Perhaps it is, but orderly in accordance with divine laws (read: "inhuman laws") that we can never quite manage to penetrate. Tlön may well be a labyrinth, but it is a labyrinth forged by men, a labyrinth destined to be deciphered by men.

Contact with Tlön, the *habit* of Tlön, has disintegrated this world. Spellbound by Tlön's rigor, humanity has forgotten, and continues to forget, that it is the rigor of chess masters, not of angels. Already Tlön's (conjectural) "primitive language" has filtered into our schools; already the teaching of Tlön's harmonious history (filled with moving episodes) has obliterated the history that governed my own childhood; already a fictitious past has supplanted in men's memories that other past, of which we now know nothing certain—not even that it is false. Numismatics, pharmacology, and archæology have been reformed. I understand that biology and mathematics are also awaiting their next avatar. . . .A scattered dynasty of recluses has changed the face of the earth—and their work continues. If my projections are correct, a hundred years from now someone will discover the hundred volumes of *The Second Encyclopædia of Tlön*.

At that, French and English and mere Spanish will disappear

---

1. There is still, of course, the problem of the *material* from which some objects are made.

from the earth. The world will be Tlön. That makes very little difference to me; through my quiet days in this hotel in Adrogué, I go on revising (though I never intend to publish) an indecisive translation in the style of Quevedo of Sir Thomas Browne's *Urne Buriall*.

The Approach to Al-Mu'tasim

Philip Guedalla writes that the novel *The Approach to Al-Mu'tasim*, by the Bombay attorney Mir Bahadur Ali, is "a rather uncomfortable amalgam of one of those Islamic allegorical poems that seldom fail to interest their translator and one of those detective novels that inevitably surpass John H. Watson's and perfect the horror of life in the most irreproachable roominghouses of Brighton." Earlier, Mr. Cecil Roberts had detected in Bahadur's book "the dual, and implausible, influence of Wilkie Collins and the illustrious twelfth-century Persian poet Farīd al-dīn Attār"; the none-too-original Guedalla repeats this calm observation, though in choleric accents. In essence, the two critics concur: both point out the detective mechanism of the novel and both speak of its mystical undercurrents. That hybridity may inspire us to imagine some similarity to Chesterton; we shall soon discover that no such similarity exists.

The first edition of *The Approach to Al-Mu'tasim* appeared in Bombay in late 1932. Its paper was virtually newsprint; its cover announced to the buyer that this was "the first detective novel written by a native of Bombay City." Within months, readers had bought out four printings of a thousand copies each. The *Bombay Quarterly Review*, the *Bombay Gazette*, the *Calcutta Review*, the *Hindustan Review* of Allahabad, and the *Calcutta Englishman* rained dithyrambs upon it. It was then that Bahadur published an illustrated edition he titled *The Conversation with the Man Called Al-Mu'tasim* and coyly subtitled *A Game with Shifting Mirrors*. That edition has just been reprinted in London by Victor Gollancz with a foreword by Dorothy L. Sayers, but with the (perhaps merciful) omission of the illustrations. I have that book before me; I have not been able to come upon the first, which I suspect is greatly superior. I am supported in this conclusion by an appendix that details the fundamental difference between the original, 1932, version and the edition of 1934. Before examining the work (and discussing it), I think it would be a good idea to give a brief general outline of the novel.

Its visible protagonist, whose name we are never told, is a law student in Bombay. In the most blasphemous way he has renounced the Islamic faith of his parents, but as the tenth night of the moon of Muharram wanes he finds himself at the center of a riot, a street battle between Muslims and Hindus. It is a night of tambours and invocations; through the inimical multitude, the great paper baldachins of the Muslim procession make their way. A Hindu brick flies from a rooftop nearby; someone buries a dagger in a belly; someone—a Muslim? a Hindu?—dies and is trampled underfoot. Three thousand men do battle—cane against revolver, obscenity against imprecation, God the indivisible against the gods. In a sort of daze, the freethinking law student enters the fray. With desperate hands, he kills (or thinks he has killed), a Hindu. Thundering, horse-borne, half asleep, the Sirkar police intervene with impartial lashes of their crops. Virtually under the hooves of the horses, the student makes his escape, fleeing toward the outermost suburbs of the city. He crosses two railroad tracks, or twice crosses the same track. He scales the wall of an unkempt garden, which has a circular tower toward the rear. A "lean and evil mob of moon-coloured hounds" emerges from the black rosebushes. Fearing for his life, the law student seeks refuge in the tower. He climbs an iron ladder—some rungs are missing—and on the flat roof, which has a pitch-black hole in the center, he comes upon a filthy man squatting in the moonlight, pouring forth a vigorous stream of urine. This man confides to the law student that it is his profession to steal the gold teeth from the cadavers the Parsees bring, swaddled in white, to that tower. He makes several further gruesome remarks and then mentions that it has been fourteen nights since he purified himself with ox dung. He speaks with obvious anger about certain Gujarati horse thieves, "eaters of dog meat and lizard meat— men, in a word, as vile as you and I." The sky is growing light; there is a lowering circle of fat vultures in the air. The law student, exhausted, falls asleep; when he awakens, the sun now high, the thief has disappeared. A couple of cigarettes from Trichinopolis have also disappeared, as have a few silver rupees. In the face of the menace that looms from the previous night, the law student decides to lose himself in India. He reflects that he has shown himself capable of killing an idolater, yet incapable of knowing with any certainty whether the Muslim possesses more of truth than the idolater does. The name Gujarat has remained with him, as has that of a *malka-sansi* (a woman of the caste of thieves) in Palanpur, a woman favored by the imprecations and hatred of the corpse-robber. The law student reasons that the wrath and hatred of a man so thoroughly despicable is the equivalent of a hymn of praise. He resolves, therefore, though with little hope, to find this woman. He performs his prayers, and then he sets out, with sure, slow steps, on the long path. That brings the reader to the end of the second chapter of the book.

It would be impossible to trace the adventures of the remaining nineteen chapters. There is a dizzying pullulation of *dramatis personæ*—not to mention a biography that seems to catalog every motion of the human spirit (from iniquity to mathematical specu- lation) and a pilgrimage that covers the vast geography of Hindustan. The story begun in Bombay continues in the lowlands of Palanpur, pauses for a night and a day at the stone gate of Bikanir, narrates the death of a blind astrologer in a cesspool in Benares, conspires in the multiform palace at Katmandu, prays and fornicates in the pestilential stench of the Machua bazaar in

Calcutta, watches the day being born out of the sea from a scribe's stool in Madras, watches the evening decline into the sea from a balcony in the state of Travancor, gutters and dies in Hindapur, and closes its circle of leagues and years in Bombay again, a few steps from the garden of those "moon-coloured" hounds. The plot itself is this: A man (the unbelieving, fleeing law student we have met) falls among people of the lowest, vilest sort and accommodates himself to them, in a kind of contest of iniquity. Suddenly—with the miraculous shock of Crusoe when he sees that human footprint in the sand—the law student perceives some mitigation of the evil: a moment of tenderness, of exaltation, of silence, in one of the abominable men. "It was as though a more complex interlocutor had spoken." He knows that the wretch with whom he is conversing is incapable of that momentary decency; thus the law student hypothesizes that the vile man before him has reflected a friend, or the friend of a friend. Rethinking the problem, he comes to a mysterious conclusion: *Somewhere in the world there is a man from whom this clarity, this brightness, emanates; somewhere in the world there is a man who is equal to this brightness.* The law student resolves to devote his life to searching out that man.

Thus we begin to see the book's general scheme: The insatiable search for a soul by means of the delicate glimmerings or reflections this soul has left in others—at first, the faint trace of a smile or a word; toward the last, the varied and growing splendors of intelligence, imagination, and goodness. The more closely the men interrogated by the law student have known Al-Mu'tasim, the greater is their portion of divinity, but the reader knows that they themselves are but mirrors. A technical mathematical formula is applicable here: Bahadur's heavily freighted novel is an ascending progression whose final term is the sensed or foreapprehended "man called Al-Mu'tasim." The person immediately preceding Al-Mu'tasim is a Persian bookseller of great courtesy and felicity; the man preceding the bookseller is a saint. . . . After all those years, the law student comes to a gallery "at the end of which there is a doorway and a tawdry curtain of many beads, and behind that, a glowing light." The law student claps his hands once, twice, and calls out for Al-Mu'tasim. A man's voice—the incredible voice of Al-Mu'tasim—bids the law student enter. The law student draws back the bead curtain and steps into the room. At that point, the novel ends.

I believe I am correct in saying that if an author is to pull off such a plot, he is under two obligations: First, he must invent a variety of prophetic signs; second, he must not allow the hero prefigured by those signs to become a mere phantasm or convention. Bahadur meets the first obligation; I am not sure to what extent he meets the second. In other words: The unheard and unseen Al-Mu'tasim should impress us as being a real person, not some jumble of vapid superlatives. In the 1932 version of the novel, the supernatural notes are few and far between; "the man called Al-Mu'tasim" has his touch of symbolism, but he possesses idiosyncratic personal traits as well. Unfortunately, that commendable literary practice was not to be followed in the second edition. In the 1934 version—the edition I have before me even now—the novel sinks into allegory: Al-Mu'tasim is an emblem of God, and the detailed itineraries of the hero are somehow the progress of the soul in its ascent to mystical plenitude. There are distressing details: A black Jew from Cochin, describing Al-Mu'tasim, says that his skin is dark; a Christian says that he stands upon a tower with his arms outspread; a red lama recalls him as seated "like that image which I carved from yak ghee and worshipped in the monastery at Tashilhumpo." Those declarations are an attempt to suggest a single, unitary God who molds Himself to the dissimilarities of humankind. In my view, that notion is not particularly exciting. I cannot say the same for another idea, however: the idea that the Almighty is also in search of Someone, and that Someone, in search of a yet superior (or perhaps simply necessary, albeit equal) Someone, and so on, to the End—or better yet, the Endlessness—of Time. Or perhaps cyclically. The etymological meaning of "Al-Mu'tasim" (the name of that eighth Abbasid king who won eight battles, engendered eight sons and eight daughters, left eight thousand slaves, and reigned for a period of eight years, eight moons, and eight days) is "He who goes in quest of aid." In the 1932 version of the novel, the fact that the object of the pilgrimage was himself a pilgrim cleverly justified the difficulty of finding Al-Mu'tasim; in the 1934 edition, that fact leads to the extravagant theology I have described. Mir Bahadur Ali, as we have seen, is incapable of resisting that basest of art's temptations: the temptation to be a genius.

I reread what I have just written and I fear I have not made sufficiently explicit the virtues of this book. It has some quite civilized features; for example, that argument in Chapter XIX in which the law student (and the reader) sense that one of the participants in the debate is a friend of Al-Mu'tasim—the man does not rebut another man's sophisms "in order not to gloat at the other man's defeat."

It is generally understood that a modern-day book may honorably be based upon an older one, especially since, as Dr. Johnson observed, no man likes owing anything to his contemporaries. The repeated but irrelevant points of congruence between Joyce's *Ulysses* and Homer's *Odyssey* continue to attract (though I shall never understand why) the dazzled admiration of critics. The points of congruence between Bahadur's novel and Farīd al-dīn Attār's classic *Conference of the Birds* meet with the no less mysterious praise of London, and even of Allahabad and Calcutta. There are other debts, as well. One investigator has documented certain analogies between the first scene of the novel and Kipling's story "On the City Wall"; Bahadur acknowledges these echoes, but claims that it would be most unusual if two portraits of the tenth night of Muharram should *not* agree. . . . With greater justice,

31

Eliot recalls that never once in the seventy cantos of Spenser's unfinished allegory *The Faërie Queene* does the heroine Gloriana appear—an omission for which Richard William Church had criticized the work. I myself, in all humility, would point out a distant, possible precursor: the Kabbalist Isaac Luria, who in Jerusalem, in the sixteenth century, revealed that the soul of an ancestor or teacher may enter into the soul of an unhappy or unfortunate man, to comfort or instruct him. That type of metempsychosis is called *ibbûr*.[1]

1. In the course of this article, I have referred to the *Mantïq al-tair*, or *Conference* [perhaps "*Parliament*"] *of the Birds*, by the Persian mystic poet Farïd al-dïn Abï Hâmid Muhammad ben Ibrâhïm (known as Attâr, or "perfumer"), who was murdered by the soldiers under Tuluy, the son of Genghis Khan, when Nishapur was sacked. Perhaps I should summarize that poem. One of the splendid feathers of the distant King of the Birds, the Sïmurgh, falls into the center of China; other birds, weary with the present state of anarchy, resolve to find this king. They know that the name of their king means "thirty birds"; they know that his palace is in the Mountains of Kaf, the mountains that encircle the earth. The birds undertake the almost infinite adventure. They cross seven *wadis* or seven seas; the penultimate of these is called Vertigo; the last, Annihilation. Many of the pilgrims abandon the quest; others perish on the journey. At the end, thirty birds, purified by their travails, come to the mountain on which the Sïmurgh lives, and they look upon their king at last: they see that they are the Sïmurgh and that the Sïmurgh is each, and all, of them. (Plotinus, too, in the *Enneads* [V, 8, 4], remarks upon a paradisal extension of the principle of identity: "Everything in the intelligible heavens is everywhere. Any thing is all things. The sun is all stars, and each star is all stars and the sun.") The *Mantïq al-tâir* has been translated into French by Garcin de Tassy, into English by Edward FitzGerald; for this note I have consulted Richard Burton's *1001 Nights*, Vol. X, and the Margaret Smith study entitled *The Persian Mystics: Attar* (1932).

The parallels between this poem and Mir Bahadur Ali's novel are not overdone. In Chapter XX, a few words attributed by a Persian bookseller to Al-Mu'tasim are perhaps an expansion of words spoken by the hero; that and other ambiguous similarities may signal the identity of the seeker and the sought; they may also signal that the sought has already influenced the seeker. Another chapter suggests that Al-Mu'tasim is the "Hindu" that the law student thinks he murdered.

Pierre Menard, Author
of the Quixote

For Silvina Ocampo

The visible œuvre left by this novelist can be easily and briefly enumerated; unpardonable, therefore, are the omissions and additions perpetrated by Mme. Henri Bachelier in a deceitful catalog that a certain newspaper, whose Protestant leanings are surely no secret, has been so inconsiderate as to inflict upon that newspaper's deplorable readers—few and Calvinist (if not Masonic and circumcised) though they be. Menard's true friends have greeted that catalog with alarm, and even with a degree of sadness. One might note that only yesterday were we gathered before his marmoreal place of rest, among the dreary cypresses, and already Error is attempting to tarnish his bright Memory. . . . Most decidedly, a brief rectification is imperative.

I am aware that it is easy enough to call my own scant authority into question. I hope, nonetheless, that I shall not be prohibited from mentioning two high testimonials. The baroness de Bacourt (at whose unforgettable *vendredis* I had the honor to meet the mourned-for poet) has been so kind as to approve the lines that follow. Likewise, the countess de Bagnoregio, one of the rarest and most cultured spirits of the principality of Monaco (now of Pittsburgh, Pennsylvania, following her recent marriage to the international philanthropist Simon Kautzsch—a man, it grieves me to say, vilified and slandered by the victims of his disinterested operations), has sacrificed "to truth and to death" (as she herself has phrased it) the noble reserve that is the mark of her distinction, and in an open letter, published in the magazine *Luxe*, bestows upon me her blessing. Those commendations are sufficient, I should think.

I have said that the *visible* product of Menard's pen is easily enumerated. Having examined his personal files with the greatest care, I have established that his body of work consists of the following pieces:

a) a symbolist sonnet that appeared twice (with variants) in the review *La Conque* (in the numbers for March and October, 1899);

b) a monograph on the possibility of constructing a poetic vocabulary from concepts that are neither synonyms nor periphrastic locutions for the concepts that inform common speech, "but are, rather, ideal objects created by convention essentially for the needs of poetry" (Nîmes, 1901);

c) a monograph on "certain connections or affinities" between the philosophies of Descartes, Leibniz, and John Wilkins (Nîmes, 1903);

d) a monograph on Leibniz' *Characteristica universalis* (Nîmes, 1904);

e) a technical article on the possibility of enriching the game of chess by eliminating one of the rook's pawns (Menard proposes, recommends, debates, and finally rejects this innovation);

f) a monograph on Ramon Lull's *Ars magna generalis* (Nîmes, 1906);

g) a translation, with introduction and notes, of Ruy López de Segura's *Libro de la invención liberal y arte del juego del axedrez* (Paris, 1907);

h) drafts of a monograph on George Boole's symbolic logic;

i) a study of the essential metrical rules of French prose, illustrated with examples taken from Saint-Simon (*Revue des langues romanes*, Montpellier, October 1909);

j) a reply to Luc Durtain (who had countered that no such

rules existed), illustrated with examples taken from Luc Durtain (*Revue des langues romanes*, Montpellier, December 1909);

k) a manuscript translation of Quevedo's *Aguja de navegar cultos*, titled *La boussole des précieux*;

l) a foreword to the catalog of an exhibit of lithographs by Carolus Hourcade (Nîmes, 1914);

m) a work entitled *Les problèmes d'un problème* (Paris, 1917), which discusses in chronological order the solutions to the famous problem of Achilles and the tortoise (two editions of this work have so far appeared; the second bears an epigraph consisting of Leibniz' advice "*Ne craignez point, monsieur, la tortue,*" and brings up to date the chapters devoted to Russell and Descartes);

n) a dogged analysis of the "syntactical habits" of Toulet (*NRF*, March 1921) (Menard, I recall, affirmed that censure and praise were sentimental operations that bore not the slightest resemblance to criticism);

o) a transposition into alexandrines of Paul Valéry's *Cimetière marin* (*N.R.F.*, January 1928);

p) a diatribe against Paul Valéry, in Jacques Reboul's *Feuilles pour la suppression de la realité* (which diatribe, I might add parenthetically, states the exact reverse of Menard's true opinion of Valéry; Valéry understood this, and the two men's friendship was never imperiled);

q) a "definition" of the countess de Bagnoregio, in the "triumphant volume" (the phrase is that of another contributor, Gabriele d'Annunzio) published each year by that lady to rectify the inevitable biases of the popular press and to present "to the world and all of Italy" a true picture of her person, which was so exposed (by reason of her beauty and her bearing) to erroneous and/or hasty interpretations;

r) a cycle of admirable sonnets dedicated to the baroness de Bacourt (1934);

s) a handwritten list of lines of poetry that owe their excellence to punctuation.[1]

This is the full extent (save for a few vague sonnets of occasion destined for Mme. Henri Bachelier's hospitable, or greedy, *album des souvenirs*) of the *visible* lifework of Pierre Menard, in proper chronological order. I shall turn now to the other, the subterranean, the interminably heroic production—the *œuvre nonpareil*, the *œuvre* that must remain—for such are our human limitations!—unfinished. This work, perhaps the most significant writing of our time, consists of the ninth and thirty-eighth chapters of Part I of *Don Quixote* and a fragment of Chapter XXII. I know that such a claim is on the face of it absurd; justifying that "absurdity" shall be the primary object of this note.[2]

Two texts, of distinctly unequal value, inspired the undertaking. One was that philological fragment by Novalis—number 2005 in the Dresden edition, to be precise—which outlines the notion of *total identification* with a given author. The other was one of those parasitic books that set Christ on a boulevard, Hamlet on La Cannabière, or don Quixote on Wall Street. Like every man of taste, Menard abominated those pointless travesties, which, Menard would say, were good for nothing but occasioning a plebeian delight in anachronism or (worse yet) captivating us with the elementary notion that all times and places are the same, or are different. It might be more interesting, he thought, though of contradictory and superficial execution, to

1. Mme. Henri Bachelier also lists a literal translation of Quevedo's literal translation of St. Francis de Sales's *Introduction à la vie dévote*. In Pierre Menard's library there is no trace of such a work. This must be an instance of one of our friend's droll jokes, misheard or misunderstood.

2. I did, I might say, have the secondary purpose of drawing a small sketch of the figure of Pierre Menard—but how dare I compete with the gilded pages I am told the baroness de Bacourt is even now preparing, or with the delicate sharp *crayon* of Carolus Hourcade?

attempt what Daudet had so famously suggested: conjoin in a single figure (Tartarin, say) both the Ingenious Gentleman don Quixote and his squire. . . .

Those who have insinuated that Menard devoted his life to writing a contemporary *Quixote* besmirch his illustrious memory. Pierre Menard did not want to compose *another* Quixote, which surely is easy enough—he wanted to compose *the* Quixote. Nor, surely, need one be obliged to note that his goal was never a mechanical transcription of the original; he had no intention of *copying* it. His admirable ambition was to produce a number of pages which coincided—word for word and line for line—with those of Miguel de Cervantes.

"My purpose is merely astonishing," he wrote me on September 30, 1934, from Bayonne. "The final term of a theological or metaphysical proof—the world around us, or God, or chance, or universal Forms—is no more final, no more uncommon, than my revealed novel. The sole difference is that philosophers publish pleasant volumes containing the intermediate stages of their work, while I am resolved to suppress those stages of my own." And indeed there is not a single draft to bear witness to that years-long labor.

Initially, Menard's method was to be relatively simple: Learn Spanish, return to Catholicism, fight against the Moor or Turk, forget the history of Europe from 1602 to 1918—*be* Miguel de Cervantes. Pierre Menard weighed that course (I know he pretty thoroughly mastered seventeenth-century Castilian) but he discarded it as too easy. Too impossible, rather!, the reader will say. Quite so, but the undertaking was impossible from the outset, and of all the impossible ways of bringing it about, this was the least interesting. To be a popular novelist of the seventeenth century in the twentieth seemed to Menard to be a diminution. Being, somehow, Cervantes, and arriving thereby at the Quixote—that looked to Menard less challenging (and therefore less interesting) than continuing to be Pierre Menard and coming to the Quixote *through the experiences of Pierre Menard*. (It was that conviction, by the way, that obliged him to leave out the autobiographical foreword to Part II of the novel. Including the prologue would have meant creating another character—"Cervantes"— and also presenting Quixote through that character's eyes, not Pierre Menard's. Menard, of course, spurned that easy solution.) "The task I have undertaken is not *in essence* difficult," I read at another place in that letter. "If I could just be immortal, I could do it." Shall I confess that I often imagine that he did complete it, and that I read the Quixote—the *entire* Quixote—as if Menard had conceived it? A few nights ago, as I was leafing through Chapter XXVI (never attempted by Menard), I recognized our friend's style, could almost hear his voice in this marvelous phrase: "the nymphs of the rivers, the moist and grieving Echo." That wonderfully effective linking of one adjective of emotion with another of physical description brought to my mind a line from Shakespeare, which I recall we discussed one afternoon:

> *Where a malignant and a turban'd Turk* ...

Why the Quixote? my reader may ask. That choice, made by a Spaniard, would not have been incomprehensible, but it no doubt is so when made by a *Symboliste* from Nîmes, a devotee essentially of Poe—who begat Baudelaire, who begat Mallarmé, who begat Valéry, who begat M. Edmond Teste. The letter mentioned above throws some light on this point. "The *Quixote*," explains Menard,

> *deeply interests me, but does not seem to me*—comment dirai-je?— *inevitable. I cannot imagine the universe without Poe's ejaculation "Ah, bear in mind this garden was enchanted!" or the* Bateau ivre *or the* Ancient Mariner, *but I know myself able to imagine it without the* Quixote. *(I am speaking, of course, of my personal ability, not of the historical resonance of those works.) The* Quixote *is a contingent work;*

the Quixote *is not necessary. I can premeditate committing it to writing, as it were—I can write it—without falling into a tautology. At the age of twelve or thirteen I read it—perhaps read it cover to cover, I cannot recall. Since then, I have carefully reread certain chapters, those which, at least for the moment, I shall not attempt. I have also glanced at the interludes, the comedies, the* Galatea, *the Exemplary Novels, the undoubtedly laborious* Travails of Persiles and Sigismunda, *and the poetic* Voyage to Parnassus. . . . *My general recollection of the* Quixote, *simplified by forgetfulness and indifference, might well be the equivalent of the vague foreshadowing of a yet unwritten book. Given that image (which no one can in good conscience deny me), my problem is, without the shadow of a doubt, much more difficult than Cervantes'. My obliging predecessor did not spurn the collaboration of chance; his method of composition for the immortal book was a bit* à la diable, *and he was often swept along by the inertiæ of the language and the imagination. I have assumed the mysterious obligation to reconstruct, word for word, the novel that for him was spontaneous. This game of solitaire I play is governed by two polar rules: the first allows me to try out formal or psychological variants; the second forces me to sacrifice them to the "original" text and to come, by irrefutable arguments, to those eradications. . . . In addition to these first two artificial constraints there is another, inherent to the project. Composing the* Quixote *in the early seventeenth century was a reasonable, necessary, perhaps even inevitable undertaking; in the early twentieth, it is virtually impossible. Not for nothing have three hundred years elapsed, freighted with the most complex events. Among those events, to mention but one, is the* Quixote *itself.*

In spite of those three obstacles, Menard's fragmentary Quixote is more subtle than Cervantes'. Cervantes crudely juxtaposes the humble provincial reality of his country against the fantasies of the romance, while Menard chooses as his "reality" the land of Carmen during the century that saw the Battle of Lepanto and the plays of Lope de Vega. What burlesque brushstrokes of local color that choice would have inspired in a Maurice Barrès or a Rodríguez Larreta*! Yet Menard, with perfect naturalness, avoids them. In his work, there are no gypsy goings-on or conquistadors or mystics or Philip IIs or *autos da fé*. He ignores, overlooks—or banishes—local color. That disdain posits a new meaning for the "historical novel." That disdain condemns *Salammbô*, with no possibility of appeal.

No less amazement visits one when the chapters are considered in isolation. As an example, let us look at Part I, Chapter XXXVIII, "which treats of the curious discourse that Don Quixote made on the subject of arms and letters." It is a matter of common knowledge that in that chapter, don Quixote (like Quevedo in the analogous, and later, passage in *La hora de todos*) comes down against letters and in favor of arms. Cervantes was an old soldier; from him, the verdict is understandable. But that *Pierre Menard's* don Quixote—a contemporary of *La trahison des clercs* and Bertrand Russell—should repeat those cloudy sophistries! Mme. Bachelier sees in them an admirable (typical) subordination of the author to the psychology of the hero; others (lacking all perspicacity) see them as a *transcription* of the Quixote; the baroness de Bacourt, as influenced by Nietzsche. To that third interpretation (which I consider irrefutable), I am not certain I dare to add a fourth, though it agrees very well with the almost divine modesty of Pierre Menard: his resigned or ironic habit of putting forth ideas that were the exact opposite of those he actually held. (We should recall that diatribe against Paul Valéry in the ephemeral Surrealist journal edited by Jacques Reboul.) The Cervantes text and the Menard text are verbally identical, but the second is almost infinitely richer. (More *ambiguous*, his detractors will say—but ambiguity is richness.)

It is a revelation to compare the *Don Quixote* of Pierre Menard with that of Miguel de Cervantes. Cervantes, for example, wrote the following (Part I, Chapter IX):

... *truth, whose mother is history, rival of time, depository of deeds, witness of the past, exemplar and adviser to the present, and the future's counselor.*

This catalog of attributes, written in the seventeenth century, and written by the "ingenious layman" Miguel de Cervantes, is mere rhetorical praise of history. Menard, on the other hand, writes:

... *truth, whose mother is history, rival of time, depository of deeds, witness of the past, exemplar and adviser to the present, and the future's counselor.*

History, the *mother* of truth!—the idea is staggering. Menard, a contemporary of William James, defines history not as a *delving into* reality but as the very *fount* of reality. Historical truth, for Menard, is not "what happened"; it is what we *believe* happened. The final phrases—*exemplar and adviser to the present, and the future's counselor*—are brazenly pragmatic.

The contrast in styles is equally striking. The archaic style of Menard—who is, in addition, not a native speaker of the language in which he writes—is somewhat affected. Not so the style of his precursor, who employs the Spanish of his time with complete naturalness.

There is no intellectual exercise that is not ultimately pointless. A philosophical doctrine is, at first, a plausible description of the universe; the years go by, and it is a mere chapter—if not a paragraph or proper noun—in the history of philosophy. In literature, that "falling by the wayside," that loss of "relevance," is even better known. The Quixote, Menard remarked, was first and foremost a pleasant book; it is now an occasion for patriotic toasts, grammatical arrogance, obscene *de luxe* editions. Fame is a form—perhaps the worst form—of incomprehension.

Those nihilistic observations were not new; what was remarkable was the decision that Pierre Menard derived from them. He resolved to anticipate the vanity that awaits all the labors of mankind; he undertook a task of infinite complexity, a task futile from the outset. He dedicated his scruples and his nights "lit by midnight oil" to repeating in a foreign tongue a book that already existed. His drafts were endless; he stubbornly corrected, and he ripped up thousands of handwritten pages. He would allow no one to see them, and took care that they not survive him.[1] In vain have I attempted to reconstruct them.

I have reflected that it is legitimate to see the "final" Quixote as a kind of palimpsest, in which the traces—faint but not undecipherable—of our friend's "previous" text must shine through. Unfortunately, only a second Pierre Menard, reversing the labors of the first, would be able to exhume and revive those Troys. . . .

"Thinking, meditating, imagining," he also wrote me, "are not anomalous acts—they are the normal respiration of the intelligence. To glorify the occasional exercise of that function, to treasure beyond price ancient and foreign thoughts, to recall with incredulous awe what some *doctor universalis* thought, is to confess our own languor, or our own *barbarie*. Every man should be capable of all ideas, and I believe that in the future he shall be."

Menard has (perhaps unwittingly) enriched the slow and rudimentary art of reading by means of a new technique—the technique of deliberate anachronism and fallacious attribution. That technique, requiring infinite patience and concentration, encourages us to read the *Odyssey* as though it came after the *Æneid*, to read Mme. Henri Bachelier's *Le jardin du Centaure* as though it were written by Mme. Henri Bachelier. This technique fills the

[1]. I recall his square-ruled notebooks, his black crossings-out, his peculiar typographical symbols, and his insect-like handwriting. In the evening, he liked to go out for walks on the outskirts of Nîmes; he would often carry along a notebook and make a cheery bonfire.

calmest books with adventure. Attributing the *Imitatio Christi* to Louis Ferdinand Céline or James Joyce—is that not sufficient renovation of those faint spiritual admonitions?

Nîmes, 1939

The Circular Ruins

And if he left off dreaming about you . . .
Through the Looking-Glass, *VI*

No one saw him slip from the boat in the unanimous night, no
one saw the bamboo canoe as it sank into the sacred mud, and
yet within days there was no one who did not know that the
taciturn man had come there from the South, and that his home-
land was one of those infinite villages that lie upriver, on the
violent flank of the mountain, where the language of the Zend is
uncontaminated by Greek and where leprosy is uncommon. But
in fact the gray man had kissed the mud, scrambled up the steep
bank (without pushing back, probably without even feeling,
the sharp-leaved bulrushes that slashed his flesh), and dragged
himself, faint and bloody, to the circular enclosure, crowned by
the stone figure of a horse or tiger, which had once been the color
of fire but was now the color of ashes. That ring was a temple
devoured by an ancient holocaust; now, the malarial jungle had
profaned it and its god went unhonored by mankind. The
foreigner lay down at the foot of the pedestal.

He was awakened by the sun high in the sky. He examined his
wounds and saw, without astonishment, that they had healed; he
closed his pale eyes and slept, not out of any weakness of the
flesh but out of willed determination. He knew that this temple
was the place that his unconquerable plan called for; he knew
that the unrelenting trees had not succeeded in strangling the

ruins of another promising temple downriver—like this one, a temple to dead, incinerated gods; he knew that his immediate obligation was to sleep. About midnight he was awakened by the inconsolable cry of a bird. Prints of unshod feet, a few figs, and a jug of water told him that the men of the region had respectfully spied upon his sleep and that they sought his favor, or feared his magic. He felt the coldness of fear, and he sought out a tomblike niche in the crumbling wall, where he covered himself with unknown leaves.

The goal that led him on was not impossible, though it was clearly supernatural: He wanted to dream a man. He wanted to dream him completely, in painstaking detail, and impose him upon reality. This magical objective had come to fill his entire soul; if someone had asked him his own name, or inquired into any feature of his life till then, he would not have been able to answer. The uninhabited and crumbling temple suited him, for it was a minimum of visible world; so did the proximity of the woodcutters, for they saw to his frugal needs. The rice and fruit of their tribute were nourishment enough for his body, which was consecrated to the sole task of sleeping and dreaming.

At first, his dreams were chaotic; a little later, they became dialectical. The foreigner dreamed that he was in the center of a circular amphitheater, which was somehow the ruined temple; clouds of taciturn students completely filled the terraces of seats. The faces of those farthest away hung at many centuries' distance and at a cosmic height, yet they were absolutely clear. The man lectured on anatomy, cosmography, magic; the faces listened earnestly, intently, and attempted to respond with understanding—as though they sensed the importance of that education that would redeem one of them from his state of hollow appearance and insert him into the real world. The man, both in sleep and when awake, pondered his phantasms' answers; he did not allow himself to be taken in by impostors, and he sensed in certain perplexities a growing intelligence. He was seeking a soul worthy of taking its place in the universe.

On the ninth or tenth night, he realized (with some bitterness) that nothing could be expected from those students who passively accepted his teachings, but only from those who might occasionally, in a reasonable way, venture an objection. The first—the accepting—though worthy of affection and a degree of sympathy, would never emerge as individuals; the latter—those who sometimes questioned—had a bit more preexistence. One afternoon (afternoons now paid their tribute to sleep as well; now the man was awake no more than two or three hours around daybreak) he dismissed the vast illusory classroom once and for all and retained but a single pupil—a taciturn, sallow-skinned young man, at times intractable, with sharp features that echoed those of the man that dreamed him. The pupil was not disconcerted for long by the elimination of his classmates; after only a few of the private classes, his progress amazed his teacher. Yet disaster would not be forestalled. One day the man emerged from sleep as though from a viscous desert, looked up at the hollow light of the evening (which for a moment he confused with the light of dawn), and realized that he had not dreamed. All that night and the next day, the unbearable lucidity of insomnia harried him, like a hawk. He went off to explore the jungle, hoping to tire himself; among the hemlocks he managed no more than a few intervals of feeble sleep, fleetingly veined with the most rudimentary of visions—useless to him. He reconvened his class, but no sooner had he spoken a few brief words of exhortation than the faces blurred, twisted, and faded away. In his almost perpetual state of wakefulness, tears of anger burned the man's old eyes.

He understood that the task of molding the incoherent and dizzying stuff that dreams are made of is the most difficult work a man can undertake, even if he fathom all the enigmas of the higher and lower spheres—much more difficult than weaving a rope of sand or minting coins of the faceless wind. He understood that initial failure was inevitable. He swore to put behind him the vast hallucination that at first had drawn him off the track, and he sought another way to approach his task. Before he began, he devoted a month to recovering the strength his delirium had squandered. He abandoned all premeditation of dreaming, and almost instantly managed to sleep for a fair portion of the day. The few times he did dream during this period, he did not focus on his dreams; he would wait to take up his task again until the disk of the moon was whole. Then, that evening, he purified himself in the waters of the river, bowed down to the planetary gods, uttered those syllables of a powerful name that it is lawful to pronounce, and laid himself down to sleep. Almost immediately he dreamed a beating heart.

He dreamed the heart warm, active, secret—about the size of a closed fist, a garnet-colored thing inside the dimness of a human body that was still faceless and sexless; he dreamed it, with painstaking love, for fourteen brilliant nights. Each night he perceived it with greater clarity, greater certainty. He did not touch it; he only witnessed it, observed it, corrected it, perhaps, with his eyes. He perceived it, he *lived* it, from many angles, many distances. On the fourteenth night, he stroked the pulmonary artery with his forefinger, and then the entire heart, inside and out. And his inspection made him proud. He deliberately did not sleep the next night; then he took up the heart again, invoked the name of a planet, and set about dreaming another of the major organs. Before the year was out he had reached the skeleton, the eyelids. The countless hairs of the body were perhaps the most difficult task. The man had dreamed a fully fleshed man—a stripling—but this youth did not stand up or speak, nor could it open its eyes. Night after night, the man dreamed the youth asleep.

In the cosmogonies of the Gnostics, the demiurges knead up a red Adam who cannot manage to stand; as rude and inept and elementary as that Adam of dust was the Adam of dream wrought from the sorcerer's nights. One afternoon, the man almost destroyed his creation, but he could not bring himself to do it. (He'd have been better off if he had.) After making vows to all the deities of the earth and the river, he threw himself at the feet of the idol that was perhaps a tiger or perhaps a colt, and he begged for its untried aid. That evening, at sunset, the statue filled his dreams. In the dream it was alive, and trembling—yet it was not the dread-inspiring hybrid form of horse and tiger it had been. It was, instead, those two vehement creatures plus bull, and rose, and tempest, too—and all that, simultaneously. The manifold god revealed to the man that its earthly name was Fire, and that in that circular temple (and others like it) men had made sacrifices and worshiped it, and that it would magically bring to life the phantasm the man had dreamed—so fully bring him to life that every creature, save Fire itself and the man who dreamed him, would take him for a man of flesh and blood. Fire ordered the dreamer to send the youth, once instructed in the rites, to that other ruined temple whose pyramids still stood downriver, so that a voice might glorify the god in that deserted place. In the dreaming man's dream, the dreamed man awoke.

The sorcerer carried out Fire's instructions. He consecrated a period of time (which in the end encompassed two full years) to revealing to the youth the arcana of the universe and the secrets of the cult of Fire. Deep inside, it grieved the man to separate himself from his creation. Under the pretext of pedagogical necessity, he drew out the hours of sleep more every day. He also redid the right shoulder (which was perhaps defective). From time to time, he was disturbed by a sense that all this had happened before. . . .His days were, in general, happy; when he closed his eyes, he would think *Now I will be with my son.* Or, less frequently, *The son I have engendered is waiting for me, and he will not exist if I do not go to him.*

Gradually, the man accustomed the youth to reality. Once he ordered him to set a flag on a distant mountaintop. The next day, the flag crackled on the summit. He attempted other, similar experiments—each more daring than the last. He saw with some bitterness that his son was ready—perhaps even impatient—to be born. That night he kissed him for the first time, then sent him off, through many leagues of impenetrable jungle, many leagues of swamp, to that other temple whose ruins bleached in the sun downstream. But first (so that the son would never know that he was a phantasm, so that he would believe himself to be a man like other men) the man infused in him a total lack of memory of his years of education.

The man's victory, and his peace, were dulled by the wearisome sameness of his days. In the twilight hours of dusk and dawn, he would prostrate himself before the stone figure, imagining perhaps that his unreal son performed identical rituals in other circular ruins, downstream. At night he did not dream, or dreamed the dreams that all men dream. His perceptions of the universe's sounds and shapes were somewhat pale: the absent son was nourished by those diminutions of his soul. His life's goal had been accomplished; the man lived on now in a sort of ecstasy. After a period of time (which some tellers of the story choose to compute in years, others in decades), two rowers woke the man at midnight. He could not see their faces, but they told him of a magical man in a temple in the North, a man who could walk on fire and not be burned.

The sorcerer suddenly remembered the god's words. He remembered that of all the creatures on the earth, Fire was the only one who knew that his son was a phantasm. That recollection, comforting at first, soon came to torment him. He feared that his son would meditate upon his unnatural privilege and somehow discover that he was a mere simulacrum. To be not a man, but the projection of another man's dream—what incomparable humiliation, what vertigo! Every parent feels concern for the children he has procreated (or allowed to be procreated) in happiness or in mere confusion; it was only natural that the sorcerer should

49

fear for the future of the son he had conceived organ by organ, feature by feature, through a thousand and one secret nights.

The end of his meditations came suddenly, but it had been foretold by certain signs: first (after a long drought), a distant cloud, as light as a bird, upon a mountaintop; then, toward the South, the sky the pinkish color of a leopard's gums; then the clouds of smoke that rusted the iron of the nights; then, at last, the panicked flight of the animals—for that which had occurred hundreds of years ago was being repeated now. The ruins of the sanctuary of the god of Fire were destroyed by fire. In the birdless dawn, the sorcerer watched the concentric holocaust close in upon the walls. For a moment he thought of taking refuge in the water, but then he realized that death would be a crown upon his age and absolve him from his labors. He walked into the tatters of flame, but they did not bite his flesh—they caressed him, bathed him without heat and without combustion. With relief, with humiliation, with terror, he realized that he, too, was but appearance, that another man was dreaming him.

The Lottery in Babylon

Like all the men of Babylon, I have been proconsul; like all, I have been a slave. I have known omnipotence, ignominy, imprisonment. Look here—my right hand has no index finger. Look here—through this gash in my cape you can see on my stomach a crimson tattoo—it is the second letter, *Beth*. On nights when the moon is full, this symbol gives me power over men with the mark of Gimel, but it subjects me to those with the Aleph, who on nights when there is no moon owe obedience to those marked with the Gimel. In the half-light of dawn, in a cellar, standing before a black altar, I have slit the throats of sacred bulls. Once, for an entire lunar year, I was declared invisible—I would cry out and no one would heed my call, I would steal bread and not be beheaded. I have known that thing the Greeks knew not— uncertainty. In a chamber of brass, as I faced the strangler's silent scarf, hope did not abandon me; in the river of delights, panic has not failed me. Heraclides Ponticus reports, admiringly, that Pythagoras recalled having been Pyrrhus, and before that, Euphorbus, and before that, some other mortal; in order to recall similar vicissitudes, I have no need of death, nor even of imposture.

I owe that almost monstrous variety to an institution—the Lottery—which is unknown in other nations, or at work in them imperfectly or secretly. I have not delved into this institution's history. I know that sages cannot agree. About its mighty purposes I know as much as a man untutored in astrology might know about the moon. Mine is a dizzying country in which the Lottery is a major element of reality; until this day, I have thought as little about it as about the conduct of the indecipherable gods or of my heart. Now, far from Babylon and its beloved customs, I think with some bewilderment about the Lottery, and about the blasphemous conjectures that shrouded men whisper in the half-light of dawn or evening.

My father would tell how once, long ago—centuries? years?—the lottery in Babylon was a game played by commoners. He would tell (though whether this is true or not, I cannot say) how barbers would take a man's copper coins and give back rectangles made of bone or parchment and adorned with symbols. Then, in broad daylight, a drawing would be held; those smiled upon by fate would, with no further corroboration by chance, win coins minted of silver. The procedure, as you can see, was rudimentary.

Naturally, those so-called "lotteries" were a failure. They had no moral force whatsoever; they appealed not to all a man's faculties, but only to his hopefulness. Public indifference soon meant that the merchants who had founded these venal lotteries began to lose money. Someone tried something new: including among the list of lucky numbers a few *unlucky* draws. This innovation meant that those who bought those numbered rectangles now had a twofold chance: they might win a sum of money or they might be required to pay a fine—sometimes a considerable one. As one might expect, that small risk (for every thirty "good" numbers there was one ill-omened one) piqued the public's interest. Babylonians flocked to buy tickets. The man who bought none was considered a pusillanimous wretch, a man with no spirit of adventure. In time, this justified contempt found a second target: not just the man who didn't play, but also the man who lost and paid the fine. The Company (as it was now beginning to be known) had to protect the interest of the winners, who could not be paid their prizes unless the pot contained almost the entire amount of the fines. A lawsuit was filed against the losers: the judge sentenced them to pay the original fine, plus court costs, or spend a number of days in jail. In order to thwart the Company, they all chose jail. From that gauntlet thrown down by a few men sprang the Company's omnipotence—its ecclesiastical, metaphysical force.

Some time after this, the announcements of the numbers drawn began to leave out the lists of fines and simply print the days of prison assigned to each losing number. That shorthand, as it were, which went virtually unnoticed at the time, was of utmost importance: *It was the first appearance of nonpecuniary elements in the lottery.* And it met with great success—indeed, the Company was forced by its players to increase the number of unlucky draws.

As everyone knows, the people of Babylon are great admirers of logic, and even of symmetry. It was inconsistent that lucky numbers should pay off in round silver coins while unlucky ones were measured in days and nights of jail. Certain moralists argued that the possession of coins did not always bring about happiness, and that other forms of happiness were perhaps more direct.

The lower-caste neighborhoods of the city voiced a different complaint. The members of the priestly class gambled heavily, and so enjoyed all the vicissitudes of terror and hope; the poor (with understandable, or inevitable, envy) saw themselves denied access to that famously delightful, even sensual, wheel. The fair and reasonable desire that all men and women, rich and poor, be able to take part equally in the Lottery inspired indignant demonstrations—the memory of which, time has failed to dim. Some stubborn souls could not (or pretended they could not) understand that this was a *novus ordo seclorum*, a necessary stage of history. . . .A slave stole a crimson ticket; the drawing determined that that ticket entitled the bearer to have his tongue burned out. The code of law provided the same sentence for stealing a lottery ticket. Some Babylonians argued that the slave

deserved the burning iron for being a thief; others, more magnani-
mous, that the executioner should employ the iron because
thus fate had decreed. . . . There were disturbances, there were
regrettable instances of bloodshed, but the masses of Babylon at
last, over the opposition of the well-to-do, imposed their will;
they saw their generous objectives fully achieved. First, the Company was forced to assume all public power. (The unification was
necessary because of the vastness and complexity of the new
operations.) Second, the Lottery was made secret, free of charge,
and open to all. The mercenary sale of lots was abolished; once
initiated into the mysteries of Baal, every free citizen automatically
took part in the sacred drawings, which were held in the labyrinths
of the god every sixty nights and determined each citizen's destiny
until the next drawing. The consequences were incalculable. A
lucky draw might bring about a man's elevation to the council of
the magi or the imprisonment of his enemy (secret, or known by
all to be so), or might allow him to find, in the peaceful dimness
of his room, the woman who would begin to disturb him, or
whom he had never hoped to see again; an unlucky draw: muti-
lation, dishonor of many kinds, death itself. Sometimes a single
event—the murder of C in a tavern, B's mysterious apotheosis—
would be the inspired outcome of thirty or forty drawings. Com-
bining bets was difficult, but we must recall that the individuals
of the Company were (and still are) all-powerful, and clever. In
many cases, the knowledge that certain happy turns were the
simple result of chance would have lessened the force of those
outcomes; to forestall that problem, agents of the Company
employed suggestion, or even magic. The paths they followed,
the intrigues they wove, were invariably secret. To penetrate the
innermost hopes and innermost fears of every man, they called
upon astrologers and spies. There were certain stone lions, a
sacred latrine called Qaphqa, some cracks in a dusty aqueduct—
these places, it was generally believed, *gave access to the Company*,
and well- or ill-wishing persons would deposit confidential

reports in them. An alphabetical file held those *dossiers* of varying veracity.

Incredibly, there was talk of favoritism, of corruption. With its customary discretion, the Company did not reply directly; instead, it scrawled its brief argument in the rubble of a mask factory. This *apologia* is now numbered among the sacred Scriptures. It pointed out, doctrinally, that the Lottery is an interpolation of chance into the order of the universe, and observed that to accept errors is to strengthen chance, not contravene it. It also noted that those lions, that sacred squatting-place, though not disavowed by the Company (which reserved the right to consult them), functioned with no official guarantee.

This statement quieted the public's concerns. But it also produced other effects perhaps unforeseen by its author. It profoundly altered both the spirit and the operations of the Company. I have but little time remaining; we are told that the ship is about to sail—but I will try to explain.

However unlikely it may seem, no one, until that time, had attempted to produce a general theory of gaming. Babylonians are not a speculative people; they obey the dictates of chance, surrender their lives, their hopes, their nameless terror to it, but it never occurs to them to delve into its labyrinthine laws or the revolving spheres that manifest its workings. Nonetheless, the semiofficial statement that I mentioned inspired numerous debates of a legal and mathematical nature. From one of them, there emerged the following conjecture: If the Lottery is an intensification of chance, a periodic infusion of chaos into the cosmos, then is it not appropriate that chance intervene in *every* aspect of the drawing, not just one? Is it not ludicrous that chance should dictate a person's death while the circumstances of that death— whether private or public, whether drawn out for an hour or a century—should *not* be subject to chance? Those perfectly reasonable objections finally prompted sweeping reform; the complexities of the new system (complicated further by its having been in practice for centuries) are understood by only a handful of specialists, though I will attempt to summarize them, even if only symbolically.

Let us imagine a first drawing, which condemns an individual to death. In pursuance of that decree, another drawing is held; out of that second drawing come, say, nine possible executors. Of those nine, four might initiate a third drawing to determine the name of the executioner, two might replace the unlucky draw with a lucky one (the discovery of a treasure, say), another might decide that the death should be exacerbated (death with dishonor, that is, or with the refinement of torture), others might simply refuse to carry out the sentence. . . .That is the scheme of the Lottery, put symbolically. *In reality, the number of drawings is infinite.* No decision is final; all branch into others. The ignorant assume that infinite drawings require infinite time; actually, all that is required is that time be infinitely subdivisible, as in the famous parable of the Race with the Tortoise. That infinitude coincides remarkably well with the sinuous numbers of Chance and with the Heavenly Archetype of the Lottery beloved of Platonists. . . .Some distorted echo of our custom seems to have reached the Tiber: In his *Life of Antoninus Heliogabalus*, Ælius Lampridius tells us that the emperor wrote out on seashells the fate that he intended for his guests at dinner—some would receive ten pounds of gold; others, ten houseflies, ten dormice, ten bears. It is fair to recall that Heliogabalus was raised in Asia Minor, among the priests of his eponymous god.

There are also *impersonal* drawings, whose purpose is unclear. One drawing decrees that a sapphire from Taprobana be thrown into the waters of the Euphrates; another, that a bird be released from the top of a certain tower; another, that every hundred years a grain of sand be added to (or taken from) the countless grains of sand on a certain beach. Sometimes, the consequences are terrible.

Under the Company's beneficent influence, our customs are

now steeped in chance. The purchaser of a dozen amphoræ of Damascene wine will not be surprised if one contains a talisman, or a viper; the scribe who writes out a contract never fails to include some error; I myself, in this hurried statement, have misrepresented some splendor, some atrocity—perhaps, too, some mysterious monotony. . . .Our historians, the most perspicacious on the planet, have invented a method for correcting chance; it is well known that the outcomes of this method are (in general) trustworthy—although, of course, they are never divulged without a measure of deception. Besides, there is nothing so tainted with fiction as the history of the Company. . . .A paleographic document, unearthed at a certain temple, may come from yesterday's drawing or from a drawing that took place centuries ago. No book is published without some discrepancy between each of the edition's copies. Scribes take a secret oath to omit, interpolate, alter. *Indirect* falsehood is also practiced.

The Company, with godlike modesty, shuns all publicity. Its agents, of course, are secret; the orders it constantly (perhaps continually) imparts are no different from those spread wholesale by impostors. Besides—who will boast of being a mere impostor? The drunken man who blurts out an absurd command, the sleeping man who suddenly awakes and turns and chokes to death the woman sleeping at his side—are they not, perhaps, implementing one of the Company's secret decisions? That silent functioning, like God's, inspires all manner of conjectures. One scurrilously suggests that the Company ceased to exist hundreds of years ago, and that the sacred disorder of our lives is purely hereditary, traditional; another believes that the Company is eternal, and that it shall endure until the last night, when the last god shall annihilate the earth. Yet another declares that the Company is omnipotent, but affects only small things: the cry of a bird, the shades of rust and dust, the half dreams that come at dawn. Another, whispered by masked heresiarchs, says that *the Company has never existed, and never will*. Another, no less despicable, argues that it makes no difference whether one affirms or denies the reality of the shadowy corporation, because Babylon is nothing but an infinite game of chance.

A Survey of the Works of Herbert Quain

Herbert Quain died recently in Roscommon. I see with no great surprise that the *Times Literary Supplement* devoted to him a scant half column of necrological pieties in which there is not a single laudatory epithet that is not set straight (or firmly reprimanded) by an adverb. The *Spectator*, in its corresponding number, is less concise, no doubt, and perhaps somewhat more cordial, but it compares Quain's first book, *The God of the Labyrinth*, to one by Mrs. Agatha Christie, and others to works by Gertrude Stein. These are comparisons that no one would have thought to be inevitable, and that would have given no pleasure to the deceased. Not that Quain ever considered himself "a man of genius"—even on those peripatetic nights of literary conversation when the man who by that time had fagged many a printing press invariably played at being M. Teste or Dr. Samuel Johnson. . . .Indeed, he saw with absolute clarity the experimental nature of his works, which might be admirable for their innovativeness and a certain laconic integrity, but hardly for their strength of passion. "I am like Cowley's odes," he said in a letter to me from Longford on March 6, 1939. "I belong not to art but to the history of art." (In his view, there was no lower discipline than history.)

I have quoted Quain's modest opinion of himself; naturally, that modesty did not define the boundaries of his thinking. Flaubert and Henry James have managed to persuade us that works of art are few and far between, and maddeningly difficult to compose, but the sixteenth century (we should recall the *Voyage to Parnassus*, we should recall the career of Shakespeare) did not share that disconsolate opinion. Nor did Herbert Quain. He believed that "great literature" is the commonest thing in the world, and that there was hardly a conversation in the street that did not attain those "heights." He also believed that the æsthetic act must contain some element of surprise, shock, astonishment— and that being astonished by rote is difficult, so he deplored with smiling sincerity "the servile, stubborn preservation of past and bygone books.". . . I do not know whether that vague theory of his is justifiable or not; I do know that his books strive too greatly to astonish.

I deeply regret having lent to a certain lady, irrecoverably, the first book that Quain published. I have said that it was a detective story— *The God of the Labyrinth*; what a brilliant idea the publisher had, bringing it out in late November, 1933. In early December, the pleasant yet arduous convolutions of *The Siamese Twin Mystery** gave London and New York a good deal of "gumshoe" work to do—in my view, the failure of our friend's work can be laid to that ruinous coincidence. (Though there is also the question—I wish to be totally honest—of its somewhat careless plotting and the hollow, frigid stiltedness of certain descriptions of the sea.) Seven years later, I cannot for the life of me recall the details of the plot, but this is the general scheme of it, impoverished (or purified) by my forgetfulness: There is an incomprehensible mur- der in the early pages of the book, a slow discussion in the middle, and a solution of the crime toward the end. Once the mystery has been cleared up, there is a long retrospective paragraph that contains the following sentence: *Everyone believed that the chessplayers had met accidentally.* That phrase allows one to infer that the solution is in fact in error, and so, uneasy, the reader looks back over the pertinent chapters and discovers *another* solution, which is the correct one. The reader of this remarkable book, then, is more perspicacious than the detective.

An even more heterodox work is the "regressive, ramifying fiction" *April March*, whose third (and single) section is dated 1936. No one, in assaying this novel, can fail to discover that it is a kind of game; it is legitimate, I should think, to recall that the author himself never saw it in any other light. "I have reclaimed for this novel," I once heard him say, "the essential features of every game: the symmetry, the arbitrary laws, the tedium." Even the name is a feeble pun: it is not someone's name, does not mean "a march [taken] in April," but literally April-March. Someone once noted that there is an echo of the doctrines of Dunne in the pages of this book; Quain's foreword prefers instead to allude to that backward-running world posited by Bradley, in which death precedes birth, the scar precedes the wound, and the wound precedes the blow (*Appearance and Reality*, 1897, p. 215).[1] But it is not the worlds proposed by *April March* that are regressive, it is the way the stories are told—regressively and ramifying, as I have said. The book is composed of thirteen chapters. The first reports an ambiguous conversation between several unknown persons on a railway station platform. The second tells of the events of the evening that precedes the first. The third, likewise retrograde, tells of the events of *another*, different, possible evening before the first; the fourth chapter relates the events of yet a third different possible evening. Each of these (mutually exclusive)

1. So much for Herbert Quain's erudition, so much for page 215 of a book published in 1897. The interlocutor of Plato's *Politicus*, the unnamed "Eleatic Stranger," had described, over two thousand years earlier, a similar regression, that of the Children of Terra, the Autochthons, who, under the influence of a reverse rotation of the cosmos, grow from old age to maturity, from maturity to childhood, from childhood to extinction and nothingness. Theopompus, too, in his *Philippics*, speaks of certain northern fruits which produce in the person who eats them the same retrograde growth. . . .Even more interesting than these images is imagining an inversion of Time itself—a condition in which we would remember the Future and know nothing, or perhaps have only the barest inkling, of the Past. *Cf. Inferno*, Canto X, ll. 97–105, in which the prophetic vision is compared to farsightedness.

"evenings-before" ramifies into three further "evenings-before,"
all quite different. The work in its entirety consists, then, of nine
novels; each novel, of three long chapters. (The first chapter is
common to all, of course.) Of those novels, one is symbolic;
another, supernatural; another, a detective novel; another, psychological; another, a Communist novel; another, anti-Communist;
and so on. Perhaps the following symbolic representation will
help the reader understand the novel's structure:

$$
z \begin{cases} y_1 \begin{cases} x_1 \\ x_2 \\ x_3 \end{cases} \\ y_2 \begin{cases} x_4 \\ x_5 \\ x_6 \end{cases} \\ y_3 \begin{cases} x_7 \\ x_8 \\ x_9 \end{cases} \end{cases}
$$

With regard to this structure, it may be apposite to say once
again what Schopenhauer said about Kant's twelve categories:
"He sacrifices everything to his rage for symmetry." Predictably,
one and another of the nine tales is unworthy of Quain; the best
is not the one that Quain first conceived, x_4; it is, rather, x_9, a tale
of fantasy. Others are marred by pallid jokes and instances of
pointless pseudoexactitude. Those who read the tales in chronological order (*e.g.*, x_3, y_1, z) will miss the strange book's peculiar
flavor. Two stories—x_7 and x_8—have no particular individual
value; it is their *juxtaposition* that makes them effective. . . . I am
not certain whether I should remind the reader that after *April
March* was published, Quain had second thoughts about the triune
order of the book and predicted that the mortals who imitated it
would opt instead for a binary scheme—

$$z \begin{cases} y_1 \begin{cases} x_1 \\ \\ x_2 \end{cases} \\ \\ y_2 \begin{cases} x_3 \\ \\ x_4 \end{cases} \end{cases}$$

while the gods and demiurges had chosen an infinite one: infinite stories, infinitely branching.

Quite unlike *April March*, yet similarly retrospective, is the heroic two-act comedy *The Secret Mirror*. In the works we have looked at so far, a formal complexity hobbles the author's imagination; in *The Secret Mirror*, that imagination is given freer rein. The play's first (and longer) act takes place in the country home of General Thrale, C.I.E., near Melton Mowbray. The unseen center around which the plot revolves is Miss Ulrica Thrale, the general's elder daughter. Snatches of dialog give us glimpses of this young woman, a haughty Amazon-like creature; we are led to suspect that she seldom journeys to the realms of literature. The newspapers have announced her engagement to the duke of Rutland; the newspapers then report that the engagement is off. Miss Thrale is adored by a playwright, one Wilfred Quarles; once or twice in the past, she has bestowed a distracted kiss upon this young man. The characters possess vast fortunes and ancient bloodlines; their affections are noble though vehement; the dialog seems to swing between the extremes of a hollow grandiloquence worthy of Bulwer-Lytton and the epigrams of Wilde or Philip Guedalla. There is a nightingale and a night; there is a secret duel on the terrace. (Though almost entirely imperceptible, there are occasional curious contradictions, and there are sordid details.) The characters of the first act reappear in the second—under different names. The "playwright" Wilfred Quarles is a traveling salesman from Liverpool; his real name is John William Quigley.

Miss Thrale does exist, though Quigley has never seen her; he morbidly clips pictures of her out of the *Tatler* or the *Sketch*. Quigley is the author of the first act; the implausible or improbable "country house" is the Jewish-Irish rooming house he lives in, transformed and magnified by his imagination. . . .The plot of the two acts is parallel, though in the second everything is slightly menacing—everything is put off, or frustrated. When *The Secret Mirror* first opened, critics spoke the names "Freud" and "Julian Green." In my view, the mention of the first of those is entirely unjustified.

Report had it that *The Secret Mirror* was a Freudian comedy; that favorable (though fallacious) reading decided the play's success. Unfortunately, Quain was over forty; he had grown used to failure, and could not go gently into that change of state. He resolved to have his revenge. In late 1939 he published *Statements*, perhaps the most original of his works—certainly the least praised and most secret of them. Quain would often argue that readers were an extinct species. "There is no European man or woman," he would sputter, "that's not a writer, potentially or in fact." He would also declare that of the many kinds of pleasure literature can minister, the highest is the pleasure of the imagination. Since not everyone is capable of experiencing that pleasure, many will have to content themselves with simulacra. For those "writers *manqués*," whose name is legion, Quain wrote the eight stories of *Statements*. Each of them prefigures, or promises, a good plot, which is then intentionally frustrated by the author. One of the stories (not the best) hints at *two* plots; the reader, blinded by vanity, believes that he himself has come up with them. From the third story, titled "The Rose of Yesterday," I was ingenuous enough to extract "The Circular Ruins," which is one of the stories in my book *The Garden of Forking Paths*.

1941

The Library of Babel

By this art you may contemplate the variation of the 23 letters . . .
Anatomy of Melancholy, *Pt. 2, Sec. II, Mem. IV*

The universe (which others call the Library) is composed of an indefinite, perhaps infinite number of hexagonal galleries. In the center of each gallery is a ventilation shaft, bounded by a low railing. From any hexagon one can see the floors above and below—one after another, endlessly. The arrangement of the galleries is always the same: Twenty bookshelves, five to each side, line four of the hexagon's six sides; the height of the bookshelves, floor to ceiling, is hardly greater than the height of a normal librarian. One of the hexagon's free sides opens onto a narrow sort of vestibule, which in turn opens onto another gallery, identical to the first—identical in fact to all. To the left and right of the vestibule are two tiny compartments. One is for sleeping, upright; the other, for satisfying one's physical necessities. Through this space, too, there passes a spiral staircase, which winds upward and downward into the remotest distance. In the vestibule there is a mirror, which faithfully duplicates appearances. Men often infer from this mirror that the Library is not infinite— if it were, what need would there be for that illusory replication? I prefer to dream that burnished surfaces are a figuration and promise of the infinite. . . .Light is provided by certain spherical fruits that bear the name "bulbs." There are two of these bulbs in each hexagon, set crosswise. The light they give is insufficient, and unceasing.

Like all the men of the Library, in my younger days I traveled; I have journeyed in quest of a book, perhaps the catalog of catalogs. Now that my eyes can hardly make out what I myself have written, I am preparing to die, a few leagues from the hexagon where I was born. When I am dead, compassionate hands will throw me over the railing; my tomb will be the unfathomable air, my body will sink for ages, and will decay and dissolve in the wind engendered by my fall, which shall be infinite. I declare that the Library is endless. Idealists argue that the hexagonal rooms are the necessary shape of absolute space, or at least of our *perception* of space. They argue that a triangular or pentagonal chamber is inconceivable. (Mystics claim that their ecstasies reveal to them a circular chamber containing an enormous circular book with a continuous spine that goes completely around the walls. But their testimony is suspect, their words obscure. That cyclical book is God.) Let it suffice for the moment that I repeat the classic dictum: *The Library is a sphere whose exact center is any hexagon and whose circumference is unattainable.*

Each wall of each hexagon is furnished with five bookshelves; each bookshelf holds thirty-two books identical in format; each book contains four hundred ten pages; each page, forty lines; each line, approximately eighty black letters. There are also letters on the front cover of each book; those letters neither indicate nor prefigure what the pages inside will say. I am aware that that lack of correspondence once struck men as mysterious. Before summarizing the solution of the mystery (whose discovery, in spite of its tragic consequences, is perhaps the most important event in all history), I wish to recall a few axioms.

First: *The Library has existed* ab æternitate. That truth, whose immediate corollary is the future eternity of the world, no rational mind can doubt. Man, the imperfect librarian, may be the work of chance or of malevolent demiurges; the universe, with its elegant appointments—its bookshelves, its enigmatic books, its indefatigable staircases for the traveler, and its water closets for the seated librarian—can only be the handiwork of a god. In order to grasp the distance that separates the human and the divine, one has only to compare these crude trembling symbols which my fallible hand scrawls on the cover of a book with the organic letters inside—neat, delicate, deep black, and inimitably symmetrical.

Second: *There are twenty-five orthographic symbols.*[1] That discovery enabled mankind, three hundred years ago, to formulate a general theory of the Library and thereby satisfactorily solve the riddle that no conjecture had been able to divine—the formless and chaotic nature of virtually all books. One book, which my father once saw in a hexagon in circuit 15–94, consisted of the letters M C V perversely repeated from the first line to the last. Another (much consulted in this zone) is a mere labyrinth of letters whose penultimate page contains the phrase *O Time thy pyramids*. This much is known: For every rational line or forthright statement there are leagues of senseless cacophony, verbal nonsense, and incoherency. (I know of one semibarbarous zone whose librarians repudiate the "vain and superstitious habit" of trying to find sense in books, equating such a quest with attempting to find meaning in dreams or in the chaotic lines of the palm of one's hand. . . .They will acknowledge that the inventors of writing imitated the twenty-five natural symbols, but contend that that adoption was fortuitous, coincidental, and that books in themselves

1. The original manuscript has neither numbers nor capital letters; punctuation is limited to the comma and the period. Those two marks, the space, and the twenty-two letters of the alphabet are the twenty-five sufficient symbols that our unknown author is referring to. [Ed. note.]

have no meaning. That argument, as we shall see, is not entirely fallacious.)

For many years it was believed that those impenetrable books were in ancient or far-distant languages. It is true that the most ancient peoples, the first librarians, employed a language quite different from the one we speak today; it is true that a few miles to the right, our language devolves into dialect and that ninety floors above, it becomes incomprehensible. All of that, I repeat, is true—but four hundred ten pages of unvarying M C V's cannot belong to any language, however dialectal or primitive it may be. Some have suggested that each letter influences the next, and that the value of M C V on page 71, line 3, is not the value of the same series on another line of another page, but that vague thesis has not met with any great acceptance. Others have mentioned the possibility of codes; that conjecture has been universally accepted, though not in the sense in which its originators formulated it.

Some five hundred years ago, the chief of one of the upper hexagons[1] came across a book as jumbled as all the others, but containing almost two pages of homogeneous lines. He showed his find to a traveling decipherer, who told him that the lines were written in Portuguese; others said it was Yiddish. Within the century experts had determined what the language actually was: a Samoyed-Lithuanian dialect of Guaraní, with inflections from classical Arabic. The content was also determined: the rudiments of combinatory analysis, illustrated with examples of endlessly repeating variations. Those examples allowed a librarian of genius to discover the fundamental law of the Library. This philosopher observed that all books, however different from one

1. In earlier times, there was one man for every three hexagons. Suicide and diseases of the lung have played havoc with that proportion. An unspeakably melancholy memory: I have sometimes traveled for nights on end, down corridors and polished staircases, without coming across a single librarian.

another they might be, consist of identical elements: the space, the period, the comma, and the twenty-two letters of the alphabet. He also posited a fact which all travelers have since confirmed: *In all the Library, there are no two identical books.* From those incontrovertible premises, the librarian deduced that the Library is "total"—perfect, complete, and whole—and that its bookshelves contain all possible combinations of the twenty-two orthographic symbols (a number which, though unimaginably vast, is not infinite)—that is, all that is able to be expressed, in every language. *All*—the detailed history of the future, the autobiographies of the archangels, the faithful catalog of the Library, thousands and thousands of false catalogs, the proof of the falsity of those false catalogs, a proof of the falsity of the *true* catalog, the gnostic gospel of Basilides, the commentary upon that gospel, the commentary on the commentary on that gospel, the true story of your death, the translation of every book into every language, the interpolations of every book into all books, the treatise Bede could have written (but did not) on the mythology of the Saxon people, the lost books of Tacitus.

When it was announced that the Library contained all books, the first reaction was unbounded joy. All men felt themselves the possessors of an intact and secret treasure. There was no personal problem, no world problem, whose eloquent solution did not exist—somewhere in some hexagon. The universe was justified; the universe suddenly became congruent with the unlimited width and breadth of humankind's hope. At that period there was much talk of The Vindications—books of *apologiæ* and prophecies that would vindicate for all time the actions of every person in the universe and that held wondrous arcana for men's futures. Thousands of greedy individuals abandoned their sweet native hexagons and rushed downstairs, upstairs, spurred by the vain desire to find their Vindication. These pilgrims squabbled in the narrow corridors, muttered dark imprecations, strangled one another on the divine staircases, threw deceiving volumes down ventilation shafts, were themselves hurled to their deaths by men of distant regions. Others went insane. . . .The Vindications do exist (I have seen two of them, which refer to persons in the future, persons perhaps not imaginary), but those who went in quest of them failed to recall that the chance of a man's finding his own Vindication, or some perfidious version of his own, can be calculated to be zero.

At that same period there was also hope that the fundamental mysteries of mankind—the origin of the Library and of time— might be revealed. In all likelihood those profound mysteries can indeed be explained in words; if the language of the philosophers is not sufficient, then the multiform Library must surely have produced the extraordinary language that is required, together with the words and grammar of that language. For four centuries, men have been scouring the hexagons. . . .There are official searchers, the "inquisitors." I have seen them about their tasks: they arrive exhausted at some hexagon, they talk about a staircase that nearly killed them—some steps were missing—they speak with the librarian about galleries and staircases, and, once in a while, they take up the nearest book and leaf through it, searching for disgraceful or dishonorable words. Clearly, no one expects to discover anything.

That unbridled hopefulness was succeeded, naturally enough, by a similarly disproportionate depression. The certainty that some bookshelf in some hexagon contained precious books, yet that those precious books were forever out of reach, was almost unbearable. One blasphemous sect proposed that the searches be discontinued and that all men shuffle letters and symbols until those canonical books, through some improbable stroke of chance, had been constructed. The authorities were forced to issue strict orders. The sect disappeared, but in my childhood I have seen old men who for long periods would hide in the latrines with metal disks and a forbidden dice cup, feebly mimicking the divine disorder.

Others, going about it in the opposite way, thought the first thing to do was eliminate all worthless books. They would invade the hexagons, show credentials that were not always false, leaf disgustedly through a volume, and condemn entire walls of books. It is to their hygienic, ascetic rage that we lay the senseless loss of millions of volumes. Their name is execrated today, but those who grieve over the "treasures" destroyed in that frenzy overlook two widely acknowledged facts: One, that the Library is so huge that any reduction by human hands must be infinitesimal. And two, that each book is unique and irreplaceable, but (since the Library is total) there are always several hundred thousand imperfect facsimiles—books that differ by no more than a single letter, or a comma. Despite general opinion, I daresay that the consequences of the depredations committed by the Purifiers have been exaggerated by the horror those same fanatics inspired. They were spurred on by the holy zeal to reach—someday, through unrelenting effort—the books of the Crimson Hexagon—books smaller than natural books, books omnipotent, illustrated, and magical.

We also have knowledge of another superstition from that period: belief in what was termed the Book-Man. On some shelf in some hexagon, it was argued, there must exist a book that is the cipher and perfect compendium *of all other books*, and some librarian must have examined that book; this librarian is analogous to a god. In the language of this zone there are still vestiges of the sect that worshiped that distant librarian. Many have gone in search of Him. For a hundred years, men beat every possible path—and every path in vain. How was one to locate the idolized secret hexagon that sheltered Him? Someone proposed searching by regression: To locate book A, first consult book B, which tells where book A can be found; to locate book B, first consult book C, and so on, to infinity. . . .It is in ventures such as these that I have squandered and spent my years. I cannot think it unlikely that there is such a total book[1] on some shelf in the universe. I pray to the unknown gods that some man—even a single man, tens of centuries ago—has perused and read that book. If the honor and wisdom and joy of such a reading are not to be my own, then let them be for others. Let heaven exist, though my own place be in hell. Let me be tortured and battered and annihilated, but let there be one instant, one creature, wherein thy enormous Library may find its justification.

Infidels claim that the rule in the Library is not "sense," but "non-sense," and that "rationality" (even humble, pure coherence) is an almost miraculous exception. They speak, I know, of "the feverish Library, whose random volumes constantly threaten to transmogrify into others, so that they affirm all things, deny all things, and confound and confuse all things, like some mad and hallucinating deity." Those words, which not only proclaim disorder but exemplify it as well, prove, as all can see, the infidels' deplorable taste and desperate ignorance. For while the Library contains all verbal structures, all the variations allowed by the twenty-five orthographic symbols, it includes not a single absolute piece of nonsense. It would be pointless to observe that the finest volume of all the many hexagons that I myself administer is titled *Combed Thunder*, while another is titled *The Plaster Cramp*, and another, *Axaxaxas mlö*. Those phrases, at first apparently incoherent, are undoubtedly susceptible to cryptographic or allegorical "reading"; that reading, that justification of the words' order and existence, is itself verbal and, *ex hypothesi*, already contained somewhere in the Library. There is no combination of characters one can make—*dhcmrlchtdj*, for example—that the divine Library has not foreseen and that in one or more of its secret tongues does

1. I repeat: In order for a book to exist, it is sufficient that it be *possible*. Only the impossible is excluded. For example, no book is also a staircase, though there are no doubt books that discuss and deny and prove that possibility, and others whose structure corresponds to that of a staircase.

not hide a terrible significance. There is no syllable one can speak that is not filled with tenderness and terror, that is not, in one of those languages, the mighty name of a god. To speak is to commit tautologies. This pointless, verbose epistle already exists in one of the thirty volumes of the five bookshelves in one of the countless hexagons—as does its refutation. (A number *n* of the possible languages employ the same vocabulary; in some of them, the *symbol* "library" possesses the correct definition "everlasting, ubiquitous system of hexagonal galleries," while a library—the thing—is a loaf of bread or a pyramid or something else, and the six words that define it themselves have other definitions. You who read me—are you certain you understand my language?)

Methodical composition distracts me from the present condition of humanity. The certainty that everything has already been written annuls us, or renders us phantasmal. I know districts in which the young people prostrate themselves before books and like savages kiss their pages, though they cannot read a letter. Epidemics, heretical discords, pilgrimages that inevitably degenerate into brigandage have decimated the population. I believe I mentioned the suicides, which are more and more frequent every year. I am perhaps misled by old age and fear, but I suspect that the human species—the *only* species—teeters at the verge of extinction, yet that the Library—enlightened, solitary, infinite, perfectly unmoving, armed with precious volumes, pointless, incorruptible, and secret—will endure.

I have just written the word "infinite." I have not included that adjective out of mere rhetorical habit; I hereby state that it is not illogical to think that the world is infinite. Those who believe it to have limits hypothesize that in some remote place or places the corridors and staircases and hexagons may, inconceivably, end—which is absurd. And yet those who picture the world as unlimited forget that the number of possible books is *not*. I will be bold enough to suggest this solution to the ancient problem: *The Library is unlimited but periodic.* If an eternal traveler should journey in any

73

direction, he would find after untold centuries that the same volumes are repeated in the same disorder—which, repeated, becomes order: the Order. My solitude is cheered by that elegant hope.[1]

Mar del Plata, 1941

---

1. Letizia Alvarez de Toledo has observed that the vast Library is pointless; strictly speaking, all that is required is a *single volume*, of the common size, printed in nine- or ten-point type, that would consist of an infinite number of infinitely thin pages. (In the early seventeenth century, Cavalieri stated that every solid body is the superposition of an infinite number of planes.) Using that silken *vademecum* would not be easy: each apparent page would open into other similar pages; the inconceivable middle page would have no "back."

The Garden of Forking Paths

For Victoria Ocampo

On page 242 of *The History of the World War*, Liddell Hart tells us that an Allied offensive against the Serre-Montauban line (to be mounted by thirteen British divisions backed by one thousand four hundred artillery pieces) had been planned for July 24, 1916, but had to be put off until the morning of the twenty-ninth. Torrential rains (notes Capt. Liddell Hart) were the cause of that delay—a delay that entailed no great consequences, as it turns out. The statement which follows—dictated, reread, and signed by Dr. Yu Tsun, former professor of English in the *Hochschule* at Tsingtao—throws unexpected light on the case. The two first pages of the statement are missing.

. . . and I hung up the receiver. Immediately afterward, I recognised the voice that had answered in German. It was that of Capt. Richard Madden. Madden's presence in Viktor Runeberg's flat meant the end of our efforts and (though this seemed to me quite secondary, or *should have seemed*) our lives as well. It meant that Runeberg had been arrested, or murdered.[1] Before the sun set on that day, I would face the same fate. Madden was implacable—

1. A bizarre and despicable supposition. The Prussian spy Hans Rabener, alias Viktor Runeberg, had turned an automatic pistol on his arresting officer, Capt. Richard Madden. Madden, in self-defense, inflicted the wounds on Rabener that caused his subsequent death. [Ed. note.]

or rather, he was obliged to be implacable. An Irishman at the orders of the English, a man accused of a certain lack of zealousness, perhaps even treason, how could he fail to embrace and give thanks for this miraculous favour—the discovery, capture, perhaps death, of two agents of the German Empire? I went upstairs to my room; absurdly, I locked the door, and then I threw myself, on my back, onto my narrow iron bed. Outside the window were the usual rooftops and the overcast six o'clock sun. I found it incredible that this day, lacking all omens and premonitions, should be the day of my implacable death. Despite my deceased father, despite my having been a child in a symmetrical garden in Hai Feng—was I, now, about to die? Then I reflected that all things happen to *oneself*, and happen precisely, precisely *now*. Century follows century, yet events occur only *in the present*; countless men in the air, on the land and sea, yet everything that truly happens, happens *to me*. . . .The almost unbearable memory of Madden's horsey face demolished those mental ramblings. In the midst of my hatred and my terror (now I don't mind talking about terror—now that I have foiled Richard Madden, now that my neck hungers for the rope), it occurred to me that that brawling and undoubtedly happy warrior did not suspect that I possessed the Secret—the name of the exact location of the new British artillery park on the Ancre. A bird furrowed the grey sky, and I blindly translated it into an aeroplane, and that aeroplane into many (in the French sky), annihilating the artillery park with vertical bombs. If only my throat, before a bullet crushed it, could cry out that name so that it might be heard in Germany. . . .But my human voice was so terribly inadequate. How was I to make it reach the Leader's ear—the ear of that sick and hateful man who knew nothing of Runeberg and me save that we were in Staffordshire, and who was vainly awaiting word from us in his arid office in Berlin, poring infinitely through the newspapers? . . . *I must flee*, I said aloud. I sat up noiselessly, in needless but perfect silence, as though Madden were already just outside my door. Something—perhaps the mere show of proving that my resources were nonexistent—made me go through my pockets. I found what I knew I would find: the American watch, the nickel-plated chain and quadrangular coin, the key ring with the compromising and useless keys to Runeberg's flat, the notebook, a letter I resolved to destroy at once (and never did), the false passport, one crown, two shillings, and a few odd pence, the red-and-blue pencil, the handkerchief, the revolver with its single bullet. Absurdly, I picked it up and hefted it, to give myself courage. I vaguely reflected that a pistol shot can be heard at a considerable distance. In ten minutes, my plan was ripe. The telephone book gave me the name of the only person able to communicate the information: he lived in a suburb of Fenton, less than a half hour away by train.

I am a coward. I can say that, now that I have carried out a plan whose dangerousness and daring no man will deny. I know that it was a terrible thing to do. I did not do it for Germany. What do I care for a barbaric country that has forced me to the ignominy of spying? Furthermore, I know of a man of England— a modest man—who in my view is no less a genius than Goethe. I spoke with him for no more than an hour, but for one hour he was Goethe. . . .No—I did it because I sensed that the Leader looked down on the people of my race—the countless ancestors whose blood flows through my veins. I wanted to prove to him that a yellow man could save his armies. And I had to escape from Madden. His hands, his voice, could beat upon my door at any moment. I silently dressed, said good-bye to myself in the mirror, made my way downstairs, looked up and down the quiet street, and set off. The train station was not far from my flat, but I thought it better to take a cab. I argued that I ran less chance of being recognised that way; the fact is, I felt I was visible and vulnerable—infinitely vulnerable—in the deserted street. I recall that I told the driver to stop a little distance from the main entrance to the station. I got down from the cab with willed and almost painful slowness. I would be going to the village of Ashgrove, but I bought a ticket for a station farther down the line. The train was to leave at eight-fifty, scant minutes away. I had to hurry; the next train would not be until nine-thirty. There was almost no one on the platform. I walked through the cars; I recall a few workmen, a woman dressed in mourning weeds, a young man fervently reading Tacitus' *Annals*, and a cheerful-looking wounded soldier. The train pulled out at last. A man I recognised ran, vainly, out to the end of the platform; it was Capt. Richard Madden. Shattered, trembling, I huddled on the other end of the seat, far from the feared window.

From that shattered state I passed into a state of almost abject cheerfulness. I told myself that my duel had begun, and that in dodging my adversary's thrust—even by forty minutes, even thanks to the slightest smile from fate—the first round had gone to me. I argued that this small win prefigured total victory. I argued that the win was not really even so small, since without the precious hour that the trains had given me, I'd be in gaol, or dead. I argued (no less sophistically) that my cowardly cheerfulness proved that I was a man capable of following this adventure through to its successful end. From that weakness I drew strength that was never to abandon me. I foresee that mankind will resign itself more and more fully every day to more and more horrendous undertakings; soon there will be nothing but warriors and brigands. I give them this piece of advice: *He who is to perform a horrendous act should imagine to himself that it is already done, should impose upon himself a future as irrevocable as the past.* That is what I did, while my eyes—the eyes of a man already dead—registered the flow of that day perhaps to be my last, and the spreading of the night. The train ran sweetly, gently, through woods of ash trees. It stopped virtually in the middle of the countryside. No one called out the name of the station. "Ashgrove?" I asked some boys on the platform. "Ashgrove," they said, nodding. I got off the train.

A lamp illuminated the platform, but the boys' faces remained within the area of shadow. "Are you going to Dr. Stephen Albert's house?" one queried. Without waiting for an answer, another of them said: "The house is a far way, but you'll not get lost if you follow that road there to the left, and turn left at every crossing." I tossed them a coin (my last), went down some stone steps, and started down the solitary road. It ran ever so slightly downhill and was of elemental dirt. Branches tangled overhead, and the low round moon seemed to walk along beside me.

For one instant, I feared that Richard Madden had somehow seen through my desperate plan, but I soon realized that that was impossible. The boy's advice to turn always to the left reminded me that that was the common way of discovering the central lawn of a certain type of maze. I am something of a *connoisseur* of mazes: not for nothing am I the great-grandson of that Ts'ui Pen who was governor of Yunan province and who renounced all temporal power in order to write a novel containing more characters than the *Hung Lu Meng* and construct a labyrinth in which all men would lose their way. Ts'ui Pen devoted thirteen years to those disparate labours, but the hand of a foreigner murdered him and his novel made no sense and no one ever found the labyrinth. It was under English trees that I meditated on that lost labyrinth: I pictured it perfect and inviolate on the secret summit of a mountain; I pictured its outlines blurred by rice paddies, or underwater; I pictured it as infinite—a labyrinth not of octagonal pavillions and paths that turn back upon themselves, but of rivers and provinces and kingdoms. . . .I imagined a labyrinth of labyrinths, a maze of mazes, a twisting, turning, ever-widening labyrinth that contained both past and future and somehow implied the stars. Absorbed in those illusory imaginings, I forgot that I was a pursued man; I felt myself, for an indefinite while, the abstract perceiver of the world. The vague, living countryside, the moon, the remains of the day did their work in me; so did the gently downward road, which forestalled all possibility of weariness. The evening was near, yet infinite.

The road dropped and forked as it cut through the now-formless meadows. A keen and vaguely syllabic song, blurred by leaves and distance, came and went on the gentle gusts of breeze. I was struck by the thought that a man may be the enemy of other men, the enemy of other men's other moments, yet not be the enemy of a country—of fireflies, words, gardens, watercourses, zephyrs. It was amidst such thoughts that I came to a high rusty gate. Through the iron bars I made out a drive lined with poplars, and a gazebo of some kind. Suddenly, I realised two things—the first trivial, the second almost incredible: the music I had heard was coming from that gazebo, or pavillion, and the music was Chinese. That was why unconsciously I had fully given myself over to it. I do not recall whether there was a bell or whether I had to clap my hands to make my arrival known.

The sputtering of the music continued, but from the rear of the intimate house, a lantern was making its way toward me—a lantern cross-hatched and sometimes blotted out altogether by the trees, a paper lantern the shape of a drum and the colour of the moon. It was carried by a tall man. I could not see his face because the light blinded me. He opened the gate and slowly spoke to me in my own language.

"I see that the compassionate Hsi P'eng has undertaken to remedy my solitude. You will no doubt wish to see the garden?"

I recognised the name of one of our consuls, but I could only disconcertedly repeat, "The garden?"

"The garden of forking paths."

Something stirred in my memory, and I spoke with incomprehensible assurance.

"The garden of my ancestor Ts'ui Pen."

"Your ancestor? Your illustrious ancestor? Please—come in."

The dew-drenched path meandered like the paths of my childhood. We came to a library of Western and Oriental books. I recognised, bound in yellow silk, several handwritten volumes of the Lost Encyclopedia compiled by the third emperor of the

Luminous Dynasty but never printed. The disk on the gramophone revolved near a bronze phoenix. I also recall a vase of *famille rose* and another, earlier by several hundred years, of that blue colour our artificers copied from the potters of ancient Persia. . . .

Stephen Albert, with a smile, regarded me. He was, as I have said, quite tall, with sharp features, grey eyes, and a grey beard. There was something priestlike about him, somehow, but something sailorlike as well; later he told me he had been a missionary in Tientsin "before aspiring to be a Sinologist."

We sat down, I on a long low divan, he with his back to the window and a tall circular clock. I figured that my pursuer, Richard Madden, could not possibly arrive for at least an hour. My irrevocable decision could wait.

"An amazing life, Ts'ui Pen's," Stephen Albert said. "Governor of the province in which he had been born, a man learned in astronomy, astrology, and the unwearying interpretation of canonical books, a chess player, a renowned poet and calligrapher—he abandoned it all in order to compose a book and a labyrinth. He renounced the pleasures of oppression, justice, the populous marriage bed, banquets, and even erudition in order to sequester himself for thirteen years in the Pavillion of Limpid Solitude. Upon his death, his heirs found nothing but chaotic manuscripts. The family, as you perhaps are aware, were about to deliver them to the fire, but his counsellor—a Taoist or Buddhist monk—insisted upon publishing them."

"To this day," I replied, "we who are descended from Ts'ui Pen execrate that monk. It was senseless to publish those manuscripts. The book is a contradictory jumble of irresolute drafts. I once examined it myself; in the third chapter the hero dies, yet in the fourth he is alive again. As for Ts'ui Pen's other labor, his Labyrinth . . ."

"Here is the Labyrinth," Albert said, gesturing towards a tall lacquered writing cabinet.

"An ivory labyrinth!" I exclaimed. "A very small sort of labyrinth . . ."

"A labyrinth of symbols," he corrected me. "An invisible labyrinth of time. I, an English barbarian, have somehow been chosen to unveil the diaphanous mystery. Now, more than a hundred years after the fact, the precise details are irrecoverable, but it is not difficult to surmise what happened. Ts'ui Pen must at one point have remarked, 'I shall retire to write a book,' and at another point, 'I shall retire to construct a labyrinth.' Everyone pictured two projects; it occurred to no one that book and labyrinth were one and the same. The Pavillion of Limpid Solitude was erected in the centre of a garden that was, perhaps, most intricately laid out; that fact might well have suggested a physical labyrinth. Ts'ui Pen died; no one in all the wide lands that had been his could find the labyrinth. The novel's confusion—confusedness, I mean, of course—suggested to me that it was that labyrinth. Two circumstances lent me the final solution of the problem—one, the curious legend that Ts'ui Pen had intended to construct a labyrinth which was truly infinite, and two, a fragment of a letter I discovered."

Albert stood. His back was turned to me for several moments; he opened a drawer in the black-and-gold writing cabinet. He turned back with a paper that had once been crimson but was now pink and delicate and rectangular. It was written in Ts'ui Pen's renowned calligraphy. Eagerly yet uncomprehendingly I read the words that a man of my own lineage had written with painstaking brushstrokes: *I leave to several futures (not to all) my garden of forking paths.* I wordlessly handed the paper back to Albert. He continued:

"Before unearthing this letter, I had wondered how a book could be infinite. The only way I could surmise was that it be a cyclical, or circular, volume, a volume whose last page would be identical to the first, so that one might go on indefinitely. I also recalled that night at the centre of the *1001 Nights*, when the queen Scheherazade (through some magical distractedness on the part of the copyist) begins to retell, verbatim, the story of the 1001 Nights, with the risk of returning once again to the night on which she is telling it—and so on, *ad infinitum.* I also pictured to myself a platonic, hereditary sort of work, passed down from father to son, in which each new individual would add a chapter or with reverent care correct his elders' pages. These imaginings amused and distracted me, but none of them seemed to correspond even remotely to Ts'ui Pen's contradictory chapters. As I was floundering about in the mire of these perplexities, I was sent from Oxford the document you have just examined. I paused, as you may well imagine, at the sentence 'I leave to several futures (not to all) my garden of forking paths.' Almost instantly, I saw it—the garden of forking paths was the chaotic novel; the phrase 'several futures (not all)' suggested to me the image of a forking in *time*, rather than in space. A full rereading of the book confirmed my theory. In all fictions, each time a man meets diverse alternatives, he chooses one and eliminates the others; in the work of the virtually impossible-to-disentangle Ts'ui Pen, the character chooses—simultaneously—all of them. *He creates*, thereby, 'several futures,' several *times*, which themselves proliferate and fork. That is the explanation for the novel's contradictions. Fang, let us say, has a secret; a stranger knocks at his door; Fang decides to kill him. Naturally, there are various possible outcomes—Fang can kill the intruder, the intruder can kill Fang, they can both live, they can both be killed, and so on. In Ts'ui Pen's novel, *all* the outcomes in fact occur; each is the starting point for further bifurcations. Once in a while, the paths of that labyrinth converge: for example, you come to this house, but in one of the possible pasts you are my enemy, in another my friend. If you can bear my incorrigible pronunciation, we shall read a few pages."

His face, in the vivid circle of the lamp, was undoubtedly that of an old man, though with something indomitable and even immortal about it. He read with slow precision two versions of a single epic chapter. In the first, an army marches off to battle through a mountain wilderness; the horror of the rocks and darkness inspires in them a disdain for life, and they go on to an easy victory. In the second, the same army passes through a palace in which a ball is being held; the brilliant battle seems to them a continuation of the *fête*, and they win it easily.

I listened with honourable veneration to those ancient fictions, which were themselves perhaps not as remarkable as the fact that a man of my blood had invented them and a man of a distant empire was restoring them to me on an island in the West in the course of a desperate mission. I recall the final words, repeated in each version like some secret commandment: "Thus the heroes fought, their admirable hearts calm, their swords violent, they themselves resigned to killing and to dying."

From that moment on, I felt all about me and within my obscure body an invisible, intangible pullulation—not that of the divergent, parallel, and finally coalescing armies, but an agitation more inaccessible, more inward than that, yet one those armies somehow prefigured. Albert went on:

"I do not believe that your venerable ancestor played at idle variations. I cannot think it probable that he would sacrifice thirteen years to the infinite performance of a rhetorical exercise. In your country, the novel is a subordinate genre; at that time it was a genre beneath contempt. Ts'ui Pen was a novelist of genius, but he was also a man of letters, and surely would not have considered himself a mere novelist. The testimony of his contemporaries proclaims his metaphysical, mystical leanings—and his life is their fullest confirmation. Philosophical debate consumes a good part of his novel. I know that of all problems, none disturbed him, none gnawed at him like the unfathomable problem of time. How strange, then, that that problem should be the *only* one that does not figure in the pages of his *Garden*. He never even uses the word. How do you explain that wilful omission?"

I proposed several solutions—all unsatisfactory. We discussed them; finally, Stephen Albert said:

"In a riddle whose answer is chess, what is the only word that must not be used?"

I thought for a moment.

"The word 'chess,'" I replied.

"Exactly," Albert said. "*The Garden of Forking Paths* is a huge riddle, or parable, whose subject is time; that secret purpose forbids Ts'ui Pen the merest mention of its name. To *always* omit one word, to employ awkward metaphors and obvious circumlocutions, is perhaps the most emphatic way of calling attention to that word. It is, at any rate, the tortuous path chosen by the devious Ts'ui Pen at each and every one of the turnings of his inexhaustible novel. I have compared hundreds of manuscripts, I have corrected the errors introduced through the negligence of copyists, I have reached a hypothesis for the plan of that chaos, I have reestablished, or believe I've reestablished, its fundamental order—I have translated the entire work; and I know that not once does the word 'time' appear. The explanation is obvious: *The Garden of Forking Paths* is an incomplete, but not false, image of the universe as conceived by Ts'ui Pen. Unlike Newton and Schopenhauer, your ancestor did not believe in a uniform and absolute time; he believed in an infinite series of times, a growing, dizzying web of divergent, convergent, and parallel times. That fabric of times that approach one another, fork, are snipped off, or are simply unknown for centuries, contains *all* possibilities. In most of those times, we do not exist; in some, you exist but I do not; in others, I do and you do not; in others still, we both do. In this one, which the favouring hand of chance has dealt me, you have come to my home; in another, when you come through my garden you find me dead; in another, I say these same words, but I am an error, a ghost."

"In all," I said, not without a tremble, "I am grateful for, and I venerate, your re-creation of the garden of Ts'ui Pen."

"Not in all," he whispered with a smile. "Time forks, perpetually, into countless futures. In one of them, I am your enemy."

I felt again that pullulation I have mentioned. I sensed that the dewdrenched garden that surrounded the house was saturated, infinitely, with invisible persons. Those persons were Albert and myself—secret, busily at work, multiform—in other dimensions of time. I raised my eyes and the gossamer nightmare faded. In the yellow-and-black garden there was but a single man—but that man was as mighty as a statue, and that man was coming down the path, and he was Capt. Richard Madden.

"The future is with us," I replied, "but I am your friend. May I look at the letter again?"

Albert rose once again. He stood tall as he opened the drawer of the tall writing cabinet; he turned his back to me for a moment. I had cocked the revolver. With utmost care, I fired. Albert fell without a groan, without a sound, on the instant. I swear that he died instantly—one clap of thunder.

The rest is unreal, insignificant. Madden burst into the room and arrested me. I have been sentenced to hang. I have most abhorrently triumphed: I have communicated to Berlin the secret name of the city to be attacked. Yesterday it was bombed—I read about it in the same newspapers that posed to all of England the enigma of the murder of the eminent Sinologist Stephen Albert by a stranger, Yu Tsun. The Leader solved the riddle. He knew that my problem was how to report (over the deafening noise of the war) the name of the city named Albert, and that the only way I could find was murdering a person of that name. He does not know (no one can know) my endless contrition, and my weariness.

Artifices
(1944)

Foreword

Although less clumsily executed, the stories in this volume are no different from those in the volume that precedes it. Two of them, perhaps, merit some comment: "Death and the Compass" and "Funes, His Memory." The second is one long metaphor for insomnia. The first, in spite of the Germanic or Scandinavian names in it, takes place in a Buenos Aires of dreams: the twisting "rue de Toulon" is the Paseo de Julio; "Triste-le-Roy" is the hotel where Herbert Ashe received, yet probably did not read, the eleventh volume of an imaginary encyclopedia. After this fiction was written, I thought it might be worthwhile to expand the time and space the story covers: the revenge might be bequeathed to others, the periods of time might be calculated in years, perhaps in centuries; the first letter of the Name might be uttered in Iceland, the second in Mexico, the third in Hindustan. Is there any need for me to say that there are saints among the Hasidim, and that the sacrifice of four lives in order to obtain the four letters that the Name demands is a fantasy dictated by the shape of my story?

Postscript, 1956. I have added three stories to this volume: "The South," "The Cult of the Phoenix," and "The End." Aside from one character, Recabarren, whose immobility and passivity serve as contrast, nothing (or almost nothing) in the brief course of that last story is of my invention—everything in it is implicit in a famous book, though I have been the first to perceive it, or at least to declare openly that I have. In the allegory of the Phoenix, I set myself the problem of suggesting a common act—the Secret—hesitatingly, gradually, and yet, in the end, unequivocally; I am not sure to what extent I have succeeded. Of "The South," which may be my best story, I shall tell the reader only that it is possible to read it both as a forthright narration of novelistic events and in quite another way, as well.

Schopenhauer, de Quincey, Stevenson, Mauthner, Shaw, Chesterton, León Bloy—this is the heterogeneous list of the writers I am continually rereading. In the Christological fantasy titled "Three Versions of Judas," I think I can perceive the remote influence of the last of these.

J.L.B.
Buenos Aires,
August 29, 1944/1956

Funes, His Memory*

I recall him (though I have no right to speak that sacred verb—only one man on earth did, and that man is dead) holding a dark passionflower in his hand, seeing it as it had never been seen, even had it been stared at from the first light of dawn till the last light of evening for an entire lifetime. I recall him—his taciturn face, its Indian features, its extraordinary *remoteness*—behind the cigarette. I recall (I think) the slender, leather-braider's fingers. I recall near those hands a *mate* cup, with the coat of arms of the Banda Oriental.* I recall, in the window of his house, a yellow straw blind with some vague painted lake scene. I clearly recall his voice—the slow, resentful, nasal voice of the toughs of those days, without the Italian sibilants one hears today. I saw him no more than three times, the last time in 1887. . . . I applaud the idea that all of us who had dealings with the man should write something about him; my testimony will perhaps be the briefest (and certainly the slightest) account in the volume that you are to publish, but it can hardly be the least impartial. Unfortunately I am Argentine, and so congenitally unable to produce the dithyramb that is the obligatory genre in Uruguay, especially when the subject is an Uruguayan. *Highbrow, dandy, city slicker*—Funes did not utter those insulting words, but I know with reasonable certainty that to him I represented those misfortunes. Pedro Leandro Ipuche* has written that Funes was a precursor of the race of supermen—"a maverick and vernacular Zarathustra"—and I will not argue the point, but one must not forget that he was also a street tough from Fray Bentos, with certain incorrigible limitations.

My first recollection of Funes is quite clear. I see him one afternoon in March or February of '84. That year, my father had taken me to spend the summer in Fray Bentos.* I was coming back from the ranch in San Francisco with my cousin Bernardo Haedo. We were riding along on our horses, singing merrily— and being on horseback was not the only reason for my cheerfulness. After a sultry day, a huge slate-colored storm, fanned by the south wind, had curtained the sky. The wind flailed the trees wildly, and I was filled with the fear (the hope) that we would be surprised in the open countryside by the elemental water. We ran a kind of race against the storm. We turned into the deep bed of a narrow street that ran between two brick sidewalks built high up off the ground. It had suddenly got dark; I heard quick, almost secret footsteps above me—I raised my eyes and saw a boy running along the narrow, broken sidewalk high above, as though running along the top of a narrow, broken wall. I recall the short, baggy trousers—like a gaucho's—that he wore, the straw-soled cotton slippers, the cigarette in the hard visage, all stark against the now limitless storm cloud. Unexpectedly, Bernardo shouted out to him—*What's the time, Ireneo?* Without consulting the sky, without a second's pause, the boy replied, *Four minutes till eight, young Bernardo Juan Francisco.* The voice was shrill and mocking.

I am so absentminded that I would never have given a second thought to the exchange I've just reported had my attention not been called to it by my cousin, who was prompted by a certain local pride and the desire to seem unfazed by the other boy's trinomial response.

He told me that the boy in the narrow street was one Ireneo Funes, and that he was known for certain eccentricities, among them shying away from people and always knowing what time it was, like a clock. He added that Ireneo was the son of a village ironing woman, María Clementina Funes, and that while some people said his father was a doctor in the salting house (an Englishman named O'Connor), others said he broke horses or drove oxcarts for a living over in the department of Salto. The boy lived with his mother, my cousin told me, around the corner from Villa Los Laureles.

In '85 and '86, we spent the summer in Montevideo; it was not until '87 that I returned to Fray Bentos. Naturally, I asked about everybody I knew, and finally about "chronometric Funes." I was told he'd been bucked off a half-broken horse on the ranch in San Francisco and had been left hopelessly crippled. I recall the sensation of unsettling magic that this news gave me: The only time I'd seen him, we'd been coming home on horseback from the ranch in San Francisco, and he had been walking along a high place. This new event, told by my cousin Bernardo, struck me as very much like a dream confected out of elements of the past. I was told that Funes never stirred from his cot, his eyes fixed on the fig tree behind the house or on a spiderweb. At dusk, he would let himself be carried to the window. He was such a proud young man that he pretended that his disastrous fall had actually been fortunate. . . .Twice I saw him, on his cot behind the iron-barred window that crudely underscored his prisonerlike state—once lying motionless, with his eyes closed; the second time motionless as well, absorbed in the contemplation of a fragrant switch of artemisia.

It was not without some self-importance that about that same time I had embarked upon a systematic study of Latin. In my suitcase I had brought with me Lhomond's *De viris illustribus*, Quicherat's *Thesaurus*, Julius Caesar's commentaries, and an odd-numbered volume of Pliny's *Naturalis historia*—a work which exceeded (and still exceeds) my modest abilities as a Latinist. There are no secrets in a small town; Ireneo, in his house on the outskirts of the town, soon learned of the arrival of those outlandish books. He sent me a flowery, sententious letter, reminding me of our "lamentably ephemeral" meeting "on the seventh of

February, 1884" He dwelt briefly, elegiacally, on the "glorious services" that my uncle, Gregorio Haedo, who had died that same year, "had rendered to his two motherlands in the valiant Battle of Ituzaingó," and then he begged that I lend him one of the books I had brought, along with a dictionary "for a full understanding of the text, since I must plead ignorance of Latin." He promised to return the books to me in good condition, and "straightway." The penmanship was perfect, the letters exceptionally well formed; the spelling was that recommended by Andrés Bello: *i* for *y*, *j* for *g*. At first, of course, I thought it was some sort of joke. My cousins assured me it was not, that this "was just . . . just Ireneo." I didn't know whether to attribute to brazen conceit, ignorance, or stupidity the idea that hard-won Latin needed no more teaching than a dictionary could give; in order to fully disabuse Funes, I sent him Quicherat's *Gradus ad Parnassum* and the Pliny.

On February 14, I received a telegram from Buenos Aires urging me to return home immediately; my father was "not at all well." God forgive me, but the prestige of being the recipient of an urgent telegram, the desire to communicate to all of Fray Bentos the contradiction between the negative form of the news and the absoluteness of the adverbial phrase, the temptation to dramatize my grief by feigning a virile stoicism—all this perhaps distracted me from any possibility of real pain. As I packed my bag, I realized that I didn't have the *Gradus ad Parnassum* and the first volume of Pliny. The *Saturn* was to sail the next morning; that evening, after dinner, I walked over to Funes' house. I was amazed that the evening was no less oppressive than the day had been.

At the honest little house, Funes' mother opened the door.

She told me that Ireneo was in the back room. I shouldn't be surprised if I found the room dark, she told me, since Ireneo often spent his off hours without lighting the candle. I walked across the tiled patio and down the little hallway farther on, and came to the second patio. There was a grapevine; the darkness seemed to me virtually total. Then suddenly I heard Ireneo's high, mocking voice. The voice was speaking Latin; with morbid pleasure, the voice emerging from the shadows was reciting a speech or a prayer or an incantation. The Roman syllables echoed in the patio of hard-packed earth; my trepidation made me think them incomprehensible, and endless; later, during the enormous conversation of that night, I learned they were the first paragraph of the twenty-fourth chapter of the seventh book of Pliny's *Naturalis historia*. The subject of that chapter is memory; the last words were *ut nihil non iisdem verbis redderetur auditum*.

Without the slightest change of voice, Ireneo told me to come in. He was lying on his cot, smoking. I don't think I saw his face until the sun came up the next morning; when I look back, I believe I recall the momentary glow of his cigarette. His room smelled vaguely musty. I sat down; I told him about my telegram and my father's illness.

I come now to the most difficult point in my story, a story whose only *raison d'être* (as my readers should be told from the outset) is that dialogue half a century ago. I will not attempt to reproduce the words of it, which are now forever irrecoverable. Instead, I will summarize, faithfully, the many things Ireneo told me. Indirect discourse is distant and weak; I know that I am sacrificing the effectiveness of my tale. I only ask that my readers try to hear in their imagination the broken and staccato periods that astounded me that night.

Ireneo began by enumerating, in both Latin and Spanish, the cases of prodigious memory cataloged in the *Naturalis historia*: Cyrus, the king of Persia, who could call all the soldiers in his armies by name; Mithridates Eupator, who meted out justice in the twenty-two languages of the kingdom over which he ruled; Simonides, the inventor of the art of memory; Metrodorus, who was able faithfully to repeat what he had heard, though it be but once. With obvious sincerity, Ireneo said he was amazed that such cases were thought to be amazing. He told me that before that rainy afternoon when the blue roan had bucked him off, he had been what every man was—blind, deaf, befuddled, and virtually devoid of memory. (I tried to remind him how precise his perception of time, his memory for proper names had been—he ignored me.) He had lived, he said, for nineteen years as though in a dream: he looked without seeing, heard without listening, forgot everything, or virtually everything. When he fell, he'd been knocked unconscious; when he came to again, the present was so rich, so clear, that it was almost unbearable, as were his oldest and even his most trivial memories. It was shortly afterward that he learned he was crippled; of that fact he hardly took notice. He reasoned (or felt) that immobility was a small price to pay. Now his perception and his memory were perfect.

With one quick look, you and I perceive three wineglasses on a table; Funes perceived every grape that had been pressed into the wine and all the stalks and tendrils of its vineyard. He knew the forms of the clouds in the southern sky on the morning of April 30, 1882, and he could compare them in his memory with the veins in the marbled binding of a book he had seen only once, or with the feathers of spray lifted by an oar on the Río Negro on the eve of the Battle of Quebracho. Nor were those memories simple—every visual image was linked to muscular sensations, thermal sensations, and so on. He was able to reconstruct every dream, every daydream he had ever had. Two or three times he had reconstructed an entire day; he had never once erred or faltered, but each reconstruction had itself taken an entire day. "*I, myself, alone, have more memories than all mankind since the world began,*" he said to me. And also: "*My dreams are like other people's waking hours.*" And again, toward dawn: "*My memory, sir, is like a garbage heap.*" A circle drawn on a blackboard, a right triangle, a rhombus—all these are forms we can fully intuit; Ireneo could do the same with the stormy mane of a young colt, a small herd of cattle on a mountainside, a flickering fire and its uncountable ashes, and the many faces of a dead man at a wake. I have no idea how many stars he saw in the sky.

Those are the things he told me; neither then nor later have I ever doubted them. At that time there were no cinematographers, no phonographs; it nevertheless strikes me as implausible, even incredible, that no one ever performed an experiment with Funes. But then, all our lives we postpone everything that can be postponed; perhaps we all have the certainty, deep inside, that we are immortal and that sooner or later every man will do everything, know all there is to know.

The voice of Funes, from the darkness, went on talking.

He told me that in 1886 he had invented a numbering system original with himself, and that within a very few days he had passed the twenty-four thousand mark. He had not written it down, since anything he thought, even once, remained ineradicably with him. His original motivation, I think, was his irritation that the thirty-three Uruguayan patriots* should require two figures and three words rather than a single figure, a single word. He then applied this mad principle to the other numbers. Instead of seven thousand thirteen (7013), he would say, for instance, "Máximo Pérez"; instead of seven thousand fourteen (7014), "the railroad"; other numbers were "Luis Melián Lafinur," "Olimar," "sulfur," "clubs," "the whale," "gas," "a stewpot," "Napoleon," "Agustín de Vedia." Instead of five hundred (500), he said "nine." Every word had a particular figure attached to it, a sort of marker; the later ones were extremely complicated. . . .I tried to explain to Funes that his rhapsody of unconnected words was exactly the opposite of a number *system.* I told him that when one said "365" one said "three hundreds, six tens, and five ones," a breakdown impossible with the "numbers" *Nigger Timoteo* or *a ponchoful of meat.* Funes either could not or would not understand me.

In the seventeenth century, Locke postulated (and condemned) an impossible language in which each individual thing—every stone, every bird, every branch—would have its own name; Funes once contemplated a similar language, but discarded the idea as too general, too ambiguous. The truth was, Funes remembered not only every leaf of every tree in every patch of forest, but every time he had perceived or imagined that leaf. He resolved to reduce every one of his past days to some seventy thousand recollections, which he would then define by numbers. Two considerations dissuaded him: the realization that the task was interminable, and the realization that it was pointless. He saw that by the time he died he would still not have finished classifying all the memories of his childhood.

The two projects I have mentioned (an infinite vocabulary for the natural series of numbers, and a pointless mental catalog of all the images of his memory) are foolish, even preposterous, but they reveal a certain halting grandeur. They allow us to glimpse, or to infer, the dizzying world that Funes lived in. Funes, we must not forget, was virtually incapable of general, platonic ideas. Not only was it difficult for him to see that the generic symbol "dog" took in all the dissimilar individuals of all shapes and sizes, it irritated him that the "dog" of three-fourteen in the afternoon, seen in profile, should be indicated by the same noun as the dog of three-fifteen, seen frontally. His own face in the mirror, his own hands, surprised him every time he saw them. Swift wrote that the emperor of Lilliput could perceive the movement of the minute hand of a clock; Funes could continually perceive the quiet advances of corruption, of tooth decay, of weariness. He saw—he *noticed*—the progress of death, of humidity. He was the solitary, lucid spectator of a multiform, momentaneous, and almost unbearably precise world. Babylon, London, and New York dazzle mankind's imagination with their fierce splendor; no one in the populous towers or urgent avenues of those cities has ever felt the heat and pressure of a reality as inexhaustible as that which battered Ireneo, day and night, in his poor South American hinterland. It was hard for him to sleep. To sleep is to take one's mind from the world; Funes, lying on his back on his cot, in the dimness of his room, could picture every crack in the wall, every molding of the precise houses that surrounded him. (I repeat that the most trivial of his memories was more detailed, more vivid than our own perception of a physical pleasure or a physical torment.) Off toward the east, in an area that had not yet been cut up into city blocks, there were new houses, unfamiliar to Ireneo. He pictured them to himself as black, compact, made of homogeneous shadow; he would turn his head in that direction to sleep. He would also imagine himself at the bottom of a river, rocked (and negated) by the current.

He had effortlessly learned English, French, Portuguese, Latin. I suspect, nevertheless, that he was not very good at thinking. To think is to ignore (or forget) differences, to generalize, to abstract. In the teeming world of Ireneo Funes there was nothing but particulars—and they were virtually *immediate* particulars.

The leery light of dawn entered the patio of packed earth.

It was then that I saw the face that belonged to the voice that had been talking all night long. Ireneo was nineteen, he had been born in 1868; he looked to me as monumental as bronze—older than Egypt, older than the prophecies and the pyramids. I was struck by the thought that every word I spoke, every expression of my face or motion of my hand would endure in his implacable memory; I was rendered clumsy by the fear of making pointless gestures.

Ireneo Funes died in 1889 of pulmonary congestion.

The Shape of the Sword

His face was traversed by a vengeful scar, an ashen and almost perfect arc that sliced from the temple on one side of his head to his cheek on the other. His true name does not matter; everyone in Tacuarembó called him "the Englishman at La Colorada." The owner of the land, Cardoso, hadn't wanted to sell it; I heard that the Englishman plied him with an argument no one could have foreseen—he told him the secret history of the scar. He had come from the border, from Rio Grande do Sul; there were those who said that over in Brazil he had been a smuggler. The fields had gone to grass, the water was bitter; to put things to right, the Englishman worked shoulder to shoulder with his peons. People say he was harsh to the point of cruelty, but scrupulously fair. They also say he liked his drink; once or twice a year he would shut himself up in the room in the belvedere, and two or three days later he would emerge as though from a battle or a spell of dizziness—pale, shaking, befuddled, and as authoritarian as ever. I recall his glacial eyes, his lean energy, his gray mustache. He was standoffish; the fact is, his Spanish was rudimentary, and tainted with the accents of Brazil. Aside from the occasional business letter or pamphlet, he got no mail.

The last time I made a trip through the northern provinces, high water along the Caraguatá forced me to spend the night at La Colorada. Within a few minutes I thought I sensed that my showing up that way was somehow inopportune. I tried to ingratiate myself with the Englishman, and to do so I seized upon patriotism, that least discerning of passions. I remarked that a country with England's spirit was invincible. My interlocutor nodded, but added with a smile that he wasn't English—he was Irish, from Dungarvan. That said, he stopped, as though he had let slip a secret.

We went outside after dinner to have a look at the sky. The clouds had cleared away, but far off behind the sharp peaks, the southern sky, creviced and split with lightning, threatened another storm. Back in the dilapidated dining room, the peon who'd served dinner brought out a bottle of rum. We drank for a long time, in silence.

I am not sure what time it was when I realized that I was drunk; I don't know what inspiration or elation or boredom led me to remark on my host's scar. His face froze; for several seconds I thought he was going to eject me from the house. But at last, his voice perfectly ordinary, he said to me:

"I will tell you the story of my scar under one condition—that no contempt or condemnation be withheld, no mitigation for any iniquity be pleaded."

I agreed. This is the story he told, his English interspersed with Spanish, and even with Portuguese:

In 1922, in one of the cities of Connaught, I was one of the many young men who were conspiring to win Ireland's independence. Of my companions there, some are still living, working for peace; others, paradoxically, are fighting under English colours, at sea or in the desert; one, the best of us all, was shot at dawn in the courtyard of a prison, executed by men filled with dreams; others (and not the least fortunate, either) met their fate in the anonymous, virtually secret battles of the civil war. We were Republicans and Catholics; we were, I suspect, romantics. For us, Ireland was not just the utopian future and the unbearable present; it was a bitter yet loving mythology, it was the circular towers and red bogs, it was the repudiation of Parnell, and it was the grand epics that sing the theft of bulls that were heroes in an earlier incarnation, and in other incarnations fish, and mountains. . . .One evening I shall never forget, there came to us a man, one of our own, from Munster—a man called John Vincent Moon.

He couldn't have been more than twenty. He was thin yet slack-muscled, all at once—he gave the uncomfortable impression of being an invertebrate. He had studied, ardently and with some vanity, virtually every page of one of those Communist manuals; he would haul out his dialectical materialism to cut off any argument. There are infinite reasons a man may have for hating or loving another man; Moon reduced the history of the world to one sordid economic conflict. He declared that the Revolution was foreordained to triumph. I replied that only *lost* causes were of any interest to a gentleman. . . .Night had fallen; we pursued our cross-purposes in the hallway, down the stairs, then through the vague streets. The verdicts Moon handed down impressed me considerably less than the sense of unappealable and absolute truth with which he issued them. The new comrade did not argue, he did not debate—he *pronounced judgement*, contemptuously and, to a degree, wrathfully.

As we came to the last houses of the city that night, we were stupefied by the sudden sound of gunfire. (Before this, or afterward, we skirted the blind wall of a factory or a gaol.) We turned down a dirt street; a soldier, huge in the glare, burst out of a torched cottage. He shouted at us to halt. I started walking faster; my comrade did not follow me. I turned around—John Vincent Moon was standing as motionless as a rabbit caught in one's headlights—eternalized, somehow, by terror. I ran back, floored the soldier with a single blow, shook Vincent Moon, cursed him, and ordered him to come with me. I had to take him by the arm; the passion of fear had stripped him of all will. But then we did run—we fled through the conflagration-riddled night. A burst of rifle fire came our way, and a bullet grazed

Moon's right shoulder; as we fled through the pine trees, a weak sob racked his breast.

In that autumn of 1922 I had gone more or less underground, and was living in General Berkeley's country house. The general (whom I had never seen) was at that time posted to some administrative position or other out in Bengal; the house was less than a hundred years old but it was gloomy and dilapidated and filled with perplexing corridors and pointless antechambers. The museum-cabinet and huge library arrogated to themselves the entire lower floor—there were the controversial and incompatible books that are somehow the history of the nineteenth century; there were scimitars from Nishapur, in whose frozen crescents the wind and violence of battle seemed to be living on. We entered the house (I think I recall) through the rear. Moon, shaking, his mouth dry, mumbled that the events of the night had been "interesting"; I salved and bandaged him, then brought him a cup of tea. The wound was superficial. Suddenly, puzzled, he stammered:

"You took a terrible chance, coming back to save me like that."

I told him it was nothing. (It was the habit of civil war that impelled me to act as I acted; besides, the imprisonment of a single one of us could imperil the entire cause.)

The next day, Moon had recovered his composure. He accepted a cigarette and subjected me to a harsh interrogation as to the "financial resources of our revolutionary party." His questions were quite lucid; I told him (truthfully) that the situation was grave. Deep rumblings of gunfire troubled the peace of the south. I told Moon that our comrades were waiting for us. My overcoat and revolver were up in my room; when I returned, I found Moon lying on the sofa, his eyes closed. He thought he had a fever; he pleaded a painful spasm in his shoulder.

It was then that I realized he was a hopeless coward. I clumsily told him to take care of himself, then left. I was embarrassed by the man and his fear, shamed by him, as though I myself were the coward, not Vincent Moon. Whatsoever one man does, it is as though all men did it. That is why it is not unfair that a single act of disobedience in a garden should contaminate all humanity; that is why it is not unfair that a single Jew's crucifixion should be enough to save it. Schopenhauer may have been right—I am other men, any man is all men, Shakespeare is somehow the wretched John Vincent Moon.

We spent nine days in the general's great house. Of the agonies and the rays of light of that dark war I shall say nothing; my purpose is to tell the story of this scar that affronts me. In my memory, those nine days form a single day—except for the next to last, when our men stormed a barracks and avenged, life for life, our sixteen comrades fallen to the machine guns at Elphin. I would slip out of the house about dawn, in the blurred confusion of first light. I would be back toward nightfall. My comrade would be waiting for me upstairs; his wound would not allow him to come down. When I look back, I see him with some book of strategy in his hand—F. N. Maude, or Clausewitz. "The weapon of preference for me," he confessed to me one night, "is artillery." He enquired into our plans; he enjoyed criticizing or rethinking them. He was also much given to deploring "our woeful financial base"; dogmatically and sombrely he would prophesy the disastrous end. "*C'est une affaire flambée*," he would mutter. To show that his physical cowardice was a matter of indifference to him, he made a great display of mental arrogance. Thus passed, well or not so well, nine days.

On the tenth, the city fell once and forever into the hands of the Black and Tans. High-sitting, silent horsemen patrolled their beats; there was ash and smoke in the wind. I saw a dead body sprawled on one corner—yet that dead body is less vivid in my memory than the dummy that the soldiers endlessly practised their marksmanship on in the middle of the city square. . . .I had gone out when dawn was just streaking the sky; before noon, I was back. Moon was in the library, talking to someone; I realized from the tone of his voice that he was speaking on the telephone. Then I heard my name; then, that I'd be back at seven, and then, that I'd be arrested as I came across the lawn. My rational friend was rationally selling me out. I heard him demand certain guarantees of his own safety.

Here my story becomes confused and peters out a bit. I know that I chased the snitch through black corridors of nightmare and steep stairwells of vertigo. Moon knew the house well, every bit as well as I. Once or twice I lost him, but I managed to corner him before the soldiers arrested me. From one of the general's suits of armor, I seized a scimitar, and with that steel crescent left a flourish on his face forever—a half-moon of blood. To you alone, Borges—you who are a stranger—I have made this confession. *Your* contempt is perhaps not so painful.

Here the narrator halted. I saw that his hands were trembling.

"And Moon?" I asked. "What became of Moon?"

"He was paid his Judas silver and he ran off to Brazil. That evening, in the city square, I saw a dummy shot by a firing squad of drunks."

I waited vainly for the rest of the story. Finally, I asked him to go on.

A groan made his entire body shiver; he gestured, feebly, gently, toward the curving whitish scar.

"Do you not believe me?" he stammered. "Do you not see set upon my face the mark of my iniquity? I have told you the story this way so that you would hear it out. It was *I* who betrayed the man who saved me and gave me shelter—it is *I* who am Vincent Moon. Now, despise me."

1942

The Theme of the Traitor and the Hero

So the Platonic Year
Whirls out new right and wrong
Whirls in the old instead;
All men are dancers and their tread
Goes to the barbarous clangour of a gong.
                    W. B. Yeats, *The Tower*

Under the notorious influence of Chesterton (inventor and embellisher of elegant mysteries) and the court counselor Leibniz (who invented preestablished harmony), in my spare evenings I have conceived this plot—which I will perhaps commit to paper but which already somehow justifies me. It needs details, rectifications, tinkering—there are areas of the story that have never been revealed to me. Today, January 3, 1944, I see it in the following way:

The action takes place in an oppressed yet stubborn country—Poland, Ireland, the republic of Venice, some South American or Balkan state. . . .Or *took* place rather, for though the narrator is contemporary, the story told by him occurred in the mid or early nineteenth century—in 1824, let us say, for convenience's sake; in Ireland, let us also say. The narrator is a man named Ryan, the great-grandson of the young, heroic, beautiful, murdered Fergus Kilpatrick, whose grave was mysteriously violated, whose name gives luster to Browning's and Hugo's verses, and whose statue stands high upon a gray hilltop among red bogs.

Kilpatrick was a conspirator and a secret and glorious captain of conspirators. Like Moses, who from the land of Moab glimpsed yet could not reach the promised land, Kilpatrick perished on the eve of the victorious rebellion he had planned for and dreamed of. The date of the first centenary of his death is approaching; the circumstances of the crime are enigmatic; Ryan, who is writing a biography of the hero, discovers that the enigma goes deeper than mere detective work can fathom. Kilpatrick was murdered in a theater; the English police never apprehended the assassin. Historians claim that this failure does not tarnish the good name of the police, since it is possible that the police themselves had Kilpatrick murdered. Other aspects of the mystery disturb Ryan; certain things seem almost cyclical, seem to repeat or combine events from distant places, distant ages. For example: Everyone knows that the constables who examined the hero's body found a sealed letter warning Kilpatrick not to go to the theater that night; Julius Caesar, too, as he was walking toward the place where the knives of his friends awaited him, received a note he never read—a note telling him of his betrayal and revealing the names of his betrayers. Caesar's wife, Calpurnia, saw in dreams a tower felled by order of the Senate; on the eve of Kilpatrick's death, false and anonymous rumors of the burning of the circular tower of Kilgarvan spread throughout the country—an event that might be taken as an omen, since Kilpatrick had been born in Kilgarvan. These (and other) parallels between the story of Julius Caesar and the story of an Irish conspirator induce Ryan to imagine some secret shape of time, a pattern of repeating lines. His thoughts turn to the decimal history conceived by Condorcet, the morphologies proposed by Hegel, Spengler, and Vico, mankind as posited by Hesiod, degenerating from gold to iron. He thinks of the transmigration of souls, a doctrine that lends horror to Celtic literature and that Caesar himself attributed to the Druids of Britain; he toys with the idea that before Fergus Kilpatrick was Fergus Kilpatrick, he was Julius Caesar. He is saved from those circular labyrinths by a curious discovery, a discovery which, however, will plunge him deep into other, yet more tangled and heterogeneous mazes: It seems that certain words spoken by a beggar who spoke with Fergus Kilpatrick on the day of his death had been prefigured by Shakespeare, in *Macbeth*. The idea that history might have copied history is mind-boggling enough; that history should copy *literature* is inconceivable. . . .Ryan digs further, and he finds that in 1814 James Alexander Nolan, the oldest of the hero's comrades, had translated Shakespeare's major plays into Gaelic—among them *Julius Caesar*. He also finds in the archives a manuscript article by Nolan on the Swiss *Festspiele*— vast peripatetic theatrical performances that require thousands of actors and retell historical episodes in the same cities, the same mountains in which they occurred. Another unpublished document reveals to Ryan that a few days before the end, Kilpatrick, presiding over the last gathering of his chiefs, had signed the death sentence of a traitor, whose name has been scratched out. This sentence does not jibe with Kilpatrick's customary mercifulness. Ryan investigates the matter (his investigation being one of the gaps in the book's narration) and manages to decipher the enigma.

Kilpatrick was murdered in a theater, yet the entire city played the role of theater, too, and the actors were legion, and the play that was crowned by Kilpatrick's death took place over many days and many nights. Here is what happened:

On August 2, 1824, the conspirators met. The country was ripe for rebellion; something, however, always went awry—there must have been a traitor within the inner circle. Fergus Kilpatrick had given James Nolan the job of ferreting out the identity of this traitor, and Nolan had carried out his mission. He announced to the gathered comrades that the traitor was Kilpatrick himself. He proved the truth of his accusation beyond the shadow of a doubt, and the men at the council that night condemned their leader to death. The leader signed his own death sentence, but he pleaded that his punishment not harm the cause.

And so it was that Nolan conceived a strange plan. Ireland idolized Kilpatrick; the slightest suspicion of his baseness would have compromised the rebellion; Nolan proposed a way to turn the traitor's execution into an instrument for the emancipation of the country. He proposed that the condemned man die at the hands of an unknown assassin in deliberately dramatic circumstances; those circumstances would engrave themselves upon the popular imagination and hasten the rebellion. Kilpatrick swore to collaborate in this plan which would give him an occasion to redeem himself, and which would be crowned by his death.

Nolan had no time to invent the circumstances of the multiple execution from scratch, and so he plagiarized the scene from another playwright, the English enemy Will Shakespeare, reprising scenes from *Macbeth* and *Julius Caesar*. The public yet secret performance occurred over several days. The condemned man entered Dublin, argued, worked, prayed, reprehended, spoke words of pathos—and each of those acts destined to shine forth in glory had been choreographed by Nolan. Hundreds of actors collaborated with the protagonist; the role of some was complex, the role of others a matter of moments on the stage. The things they did and said endure in Ireland's history books and in its impassioned memory. Kilpatrick, moved almost to ecstasy by the scrupulously plotted fate that would redeem him and end his days, more than once enriched his judge's text with improvised words and acts. Thus the teeming drama played itself out in time, until that August 6, 1824, in a box (prefiguring Lincoln's) draped with funereal curtains, when a yearned-for bullet pierced the traitor-hero's breast. Between two spurts of sudden blood, Kilpatrick could hardly pronounce the few words given him to speak.

In Nolan's play, the passages taken from Shakespeare are the *least* dramatic ones; Ryan suspected that the author interpolated them so that someone, in the future, would be able to stumble upon the truth. Ryan realized that he, too, was part of Nolan's plot. . . .After long and stubborn deliberation, he decided to silence the discovery. He published a book dedicated to the hero's glory; that too, perhaps, had been foreseen.

Death and the Compass

For Mandie Molina Vedia

Of the many problems on which Lönnrot's reckless perspicacity was exercised, none was so strange—so *rigorously* strange, one might say—as the periodic series of bloody deeds that culminated at the Villa Triste-le-Roy, amid the perpetual fragrance of the eucalyptus. It is true that Erik Lönnrot did not succeed in preventing the last crime, but he did, indisputably, foresee it. Nor did he divine the identity of Yarmolinsky's unlucky murderer, but he did perceive the evil series' secret shape and the part played in it by Red Scharlach, whose second sobriquet is Scharlach the Dandy. That criminal (like so many others) had sworn upon his honor to kill Lönnrot, but Lönnrot never allowed himself to be intimidated. He thought of himself as a reasoning machine, an Auguste Dupin, but there was something of the adventurer in him, even something of the gambler.

The first crime occurred in the Hôtel du Nord, that tall prism sitting high above the estuary whose waters are the color of the desert. To that tower (which is notorious for uniting in itself the abhorrent whiteness of a sanatorium, the numbered divisibility of a prison, and the general appearance of a house of ill repute) there came, on December 3, the delegate from Podolsk to the Third Talmudic Congress—Dr. Marcelo Yarmolinsky, a man of gray beard and gray eyes. We will never know whether he found the Hôtel du Nord to his liking; he accepted it with the ancient resignation that had allowed him to bear three years of war in the Carpathians and three thousand years of pogroms and oppression.

He was given a room on R Floor, across the hall from the suite occupied—not without some splendor—by the Tetrarch of Galilee. Yarmolinsky had dinner, put off till the next day his examination of the unfamiliar city, set out his many books and very few articles of jewelry on a bureau, and, before midnight, turned off the light. (Thus testified the tetrarch's driver, who was sleeping in the adjoining room.) On the fourth, at 11:30 AM, a writer for the *Yiddische Zeitung* telephoned Yarmolinsky, but Dr. Yarmolinsky did not answer. He was found lying on the floor of his room, his face by now slightly discolored, his body almost naked beneath an anachronistic cape. He was lying not far from the door to the hallway; a deep knife wound had rent his chest. A couple of hours later, in the same room, standing amid journalists, photographers, and gendarmes, police commissioner Treviranus and Lönnrot serenely discussed the problem.

"No need to go off on wild-goose chases here," Treviranus was saying, as he brandished an imperious cigar. "We all know that the Tetrarch of Galilee owns the finest sapphires in the world. Somebody intending to steal the sapphires broke in here by mistake. Yarmolinsky woke up, the burglar had to kill him.— What do you think?"

"Possible, but uninteresting," Lönnrot replied. "You will reply that reality has not the slightest obligation to be interesting. I will reply in turn that reality may get along without that obligation, but hypotheses may not. In the hypothesis that you suggest, here, on the spur of the moment, chance plays a disproportionate role. What we have here is a dead rabbi; I would prefer a purely rabbinical explanation, not the imaginary bunglings of an imaginary burglar."

Treviranus' humor darkened.

"I'm not interested in 'rabbinical explanations,' as you call them; what I'm interested in is catching the blackguard that stabbed this unknown man."

"Unknown?" asked Lönnrot. "Here are his complete works."

He gestured to the bureau with its row of tall books: *A Vindication of the Kabbalah; A Study of the Philosophy of Robert Fludd;* a literal translation of the *Sefer Yetsirah;* a *Biography of the Baal Shem; A History of the Hasidim;* a monograph in German on the Tetragrammaton; another on the divine nomenclature of the Pentateuch. The commissioner looked at them with fear, almost with revulsion. Then he laughed.

"I'm a poor Christian fellow," he replied. "You can take those things home with you, if you want them; I can't be wasting my time on Jewish superstitions."

"This crime may, however, *belong* to the history of Jewish superstitions," Lönnrot muttered.

"As Christianity does," the writer from the *Yiddische Zeitung* added, scathingly. He was nearsighted, quite shy, and an atheist.

No one answered him. In the little typewriter, one of the agents had found a slip of paper, with this unfinished declaration:

> *The first letter of the Name has been written.*

Lönnrot resisted a smile. Suddenly turned bibliophile or Hebraist, he ordered one of the officers to wrap up the dead man's books, and he took them to his apartment. Then, indifferent to the police investigation, he set about studying them. One book, an octavo volume, revealed to him the teachings of Israel Baal Shem Tov, the founder of the sect of the Pious; another, the virtues and terrors of the Tetragrammaton, the ineffable name of God; yet another, the notion that God has a secret name, which (much like the crystal sphere attributed by the Persians to Alexander of Macedonia) contains His ninth attribute, the eternity—that is, immediate knowledge—of all things that shall be, are, and have been in the universe. Tradition reckons the names of God at ninety-nine; while Hebraists attribute that imperfect sum to the magical fear of even numbers, the Hasidim argue that the lacuna points toward a hundredth name—the Absolute Name.

From his erudition Lönnrot was distracted, a few days later, by the writer from the *Yiddische Zeitung*. The young man wanted to talk about the murder; Lönnrot preferred to talk about the many names of God. The journalist filled three columns with the story that the famed detective Erik Lönnrot had taken up the study of the names of God in order to discover the name of the murderer. Lönnrot, accustomed to journalists' simplifications, did not take offense. One of those shopkeepers who have found that any given man may be persuaded to buy any given book published a popular edition of *A History of the Hasidim*.

The second crime took place on the night of January 3, in the emptiest and most godforsaken of the echoing suburbs on the western outskirts of the capital. Sometime around dawn, one of the mounted gendarmes that patrolled the solitudes of those blocks saw a man, wrapped in a poncho, lying in the doorway of an old paint factory. His hard face looked as though it were wearing a mask of blood; a deep knife wound split his chest. On the wall, across the red and yellow rhombuses, someone had chalked some words, which the gendarme spelled out to himself. . . .That afternoon, Treviranus and Lönnrot made their way to the distant scene of the crime. To the left and right of their automobile, the city crumbled away; the sky expanded, and now houses held less and less importance, a brick kiln or a poplar tree more and more. They came to their miserable destination; a final alleyway lined with pink-colored walls that somehow seemed to reflect the rambunctious setting of the sun. By this time, the dead man had been identified. He was Daniel Simón Azevedo, a man of some reputation in the old slums of the Northside, where he had risen from wagon driver to election-day thug, only to degenerate thereafter into a thief and even an informer. (The singular manner of his death seemed fitting: Azevedo was the last representative of a generation of outlaws who used a knife but not a revolver.) The chalked words read as follows:

The second letter of the Name has been written.

The third crime took place on the night of February 3. A few minutes before one, the telephone rang in Commissioner Treviranus' office. Keenly secretive, the guttural voice of a man came on the line; he told the commissioner his name was Ginzberg (or Ginsburg) and said that for a reasonable fee he was willing to reveal certain details of the two sacrifices, Azevedo's and Yarmolinsky's. A cacophony of whistles and party horns drowned out the informer's voice. Then, the line went dead. Without discarding the possibility of a prank (it was carnival time, after all), Treviranus made inquiries and found that the call had come from Liverpool House, a tavern on the rue de Toulon—that brackish street shared by a popular museum of wonders and a milk store, a brothel and a company of Bible sellers. Treviranus telephoned the owner of the place—Black Finnegan, former Irish criminal now overwhelmed, almost crushed, by honesty. Finnegan told Treviranus that the last person to use the telephone in the tavern had been a tenant, one Gryphius, who'd just gone out with some friends. Treviranus drove immediately to Liverpool House. The owner had the following to say: Eight days earlier, Gryphius—a man with sharp features, a nebulous gray beard, and a nondescript black suit—had rented a room above the bar. Finnegan (who generally put the room to a use that Treviranus had no difficulty guessing) had named an exorbitant rent; Gryphius had unhesitatingly paid it. He almost never left the room; he had both lunch and dinner there and hardly ever showed his face in the bar. That night he had come down to Finnegan's office to make a call. A closed coupe had stopped in front of the tavern. The driver hadn't left the driver's seat; some of the customers recalled that he was wearing a bear mask. Two harlequin figures got out of the car; they were short, and no one could fail to notice that they were drunk. They burst into Finnegan's office, party horns bleating, and threw their arms around Gryphius, who apparently recognized them but greeted them somewhat coldly. They exchanged a few words in Yiddish—Gryphius in a low, guttural voice, the harlequins in a sort of falsetto—and then all went up to Gryphius' room. Fifteen minutes later the three men came down again, quite happy; Gryphius was staggering, and seemed to be as drunk as the others. Tall and unsteady, his head apparently spinning, he was in the middle, between the masked harlequins. (One of the women in the bar recalled the yellow, red, and green lozenges.) Twice he stumbled; twice the harlequins steadied him. The three men got into the coupe and disappeared in the direction of the nearby pier, with its rectangular water. But just as he stepped on the running board of the car, the last harlequin scrawled an obscene figure and a sentence on one of the blackboards in the entryway. Treviranus looked at the sentence, but it was almost predictable:

The last letter of the Name has been written.

Then he examined Gryphius-Ginsburg's little room. On the floor, there was a brusque star, in blood; in the corners, the remains of cigarettes, Hungarian; on a bureau, a book in Latin—Leusden's *Philologus hebræogræcus* (1739)—with several handwritten notes. Treviranus looked at it indignantly, and sent for Lönnrot. Lönnrot did not take his hat off before plunging into the book, while the commissioner interrogated the contradictory witnesses to the possible kidnapping. At four they left. Out in the twisting rue de Toulon, as they walked through the dawn's dead streamers and confetti, Treviranus said:

"What if tonight's story were a sham, a simulacrum?"

Erik Lönnrot smiled and in a grave voice read the commissioner a passage (which had been underlined) from the *Philologus'* thirty-third dissertation: *Dies Judæorum incipit a solis occasu usque ad solis occasum diei sequentis.* "Which means," he added, " 'The Jewish day begins at sundown and lasts until sundown of the following day.' "

The other man made an attempt at irony.

"And is that the most valuable piece of information you've picked up tonight, then?"

"No. The most valuable piece of information is the word Ginsburg used."

The afternoon papers had not overlooked these periodic deaths and disappearances. The *Cross and Sword* contrasted them with the admirable discipline and order of the last Hermetic congress; Ernst Palast of *The Martyr* denounced "the intolerable delays of a clandestine and niggardly pogrom, which has taken three months to wipe out three Jews"; the *Yiddische Zeitung* rejected the horrifying theory of an anti-Semitic conspiracy, "though many insightful spirits will hear of no other solution for the triple mystery"; the most famous gunman of the Southside, Dandy Red Scharlach, swore that in his territory no crime such as that had ever taken place, and he accused Police Commissioner Franz Treviranus of criminal negligence.

On March 1, this same Treviranus received an impressive-looking sealed envelope. He opened it; it contained a letter signed "Baruch Spinoza" and a detailed map of the city, clearly torn out of a Baedeker. The letter predicted that on the third of March there would not be a fourth crime, because the paint factory in the west, the tavern on the rue de Toulon, and the Hôtel du Nord were "the perfect points of a mystical, equilateral triangle"; red ink on the map demonstrated its regularity. Treviranus read over that argument-by-geometry resignedly and then sent both letter and map to Lönnrot's house, Lönnrot indisputably being a man who deserved this sort of claptrap.

Erik Lönnrot studied the map and letter. The three locations were indeed equidistant. Symmetry in time (December 3, January 3, February 3); symmetry in space, as well ... Lönnrot sensed, abruptly, that he was on the brink of solving the riddle. A drawing-compass and a navigational compass completed that sudden intuition. He smiled, spoke the word Tetragrammaton (a word he had recently acquired), and telephoned the commissioner.

"Thanks for that equilateral triangle you sent me last night. It was what I needed to solve the puzzle. Tomorrow, Friday, the perpetrators will be in prison; we can relax."

"Then they're not planning a fourth crime?"

"It's precisely because they *are* planning a fourth crime that we can relax," Lönnrot said as he hung up.

An hour later, he was riding on a Southern Railway train toward the abandoned Villa Triste-le-Roy. South of the city of my story flows a sluggish stream of muddy water, choked with refuse and thick with the runoff of tanneries. On the other side is a suburb filled with factories where, under the protection of a Barcelona gangster, gunmen prosper. Lönnrot smiled to think that the most famous of these criminals—Red Scharlach—would have given anything to know about his clandestine visit. Azevedo had been one of Scharlach's gang; Lönnrot considered the remote possibility that Scharlach was to be the fourth victim, but then rejected it. . . . He had virtually solved the problem; the mere circumstances, the reality (names, arrests, faces, the paperwork of trial and imprisonment), held very little interest for him now. He wanted to go for a walk, he wanted a respite from the three months of sedentary investigation. He reflected that the explanation for the crimes lay in an anonymous triangle and a dusty Greek word. The mystery seemed so crystal clear to him now, he was embarrassed to have spent a hundred days on it.

The train stopped at a silent loading platform. Lönnrot got off. It was one of those deserted evenings that have the look of dawn. The air of the murky plains was wet and cold. Lönnrot began to walk cross-country. He saw dogs, he saw a van or lorry in a dead-end alleyway, he saw the horizon, he saw a silvery horse lapping at the rank water of a puddle. It was growing dark when he saw the rectangular belvedere of Villa Triste-le-Roy, which stood almost as high as the black eucalyptus trees that surrounded it. The thought occurred to him that one dawn and one sunset (an ancient glow in the east and another in the west) were all that separated him from the hour yearned for by the seekers of the Name.

A rusty fence defined the irregular perimeter of the villa's grounds. The main gate was closed. Lönnrot, with no great expectation of finding a way in, walked all the way around. Back at the impregnable gate, he stuck his hand almost mechanically between the bars and came upon the latch. The creaking of the iron startled him. With laborious passivity, the entire gate yielded.

Lönnrot made his way forward through the eucalyptus trees, treading upon confused generations of stiff red leaves. Seen at closer quarters, the house belonging to the Villa Triste-le-Roy abounded in pointless symmetries and obsessive repetitions; a glacial Diana in a gloomy niche was echoed by a second Diana in a second niche; one balcony was reflected in another; double stairways opened into a double balustrade. A two-faced Hermes threw a monstrous shadow. Lönnrot walked all around the outside of the house as he had made the circuit of the villa's grounds. He inspected everything; under the level of the terrace, he spotted a narrow shutter.

He pushed at it; two or three marble steps descended into a cellar. Lönnrot, who by now had a sense of the architect's predilections, guessed that there would be another set of steps in the opposite wall. He found them, climbed them, raised his hands, and opened the trapdoor out.

A glowing light led him toward a window. This he also opened; a round yellow moon defined two leaf-clogged fountains in the dreary garden. Lönnrot explored the house. Through foyers that opened onto dining rooms and on through galleries, he would emerge into identical courtyards—often the same courtyard. He climbed dusty stairs to circular antechambers; he would recede infinitely in the facing mirrored walls; he wearied of opening or half opening windows that revealed to him, outside, the same desolate garden from differing heights and differing angles—

inside, the furnishings in yellowing covers, chandeliers swathed in muslin. A bedchamber stopped him; there, a single flower in a porcelain vase; at the first brush of his fingertips, the ancient petals crumbled. On the second floor, on the uppermost floor, the house seemed infinite yet still growing. *The house is not so large,* he thought. *It seems larger because of its dimness, its symmetry, its mirrors, its age, my unfamiliarity with it, and this solitude.*

A stairway took him to the belvedere. The moonlight of the evening shone through the lozenges of the windows; they were yellow, red, and green. He was stopped by an astonished, dizzying recollection.

Two fierce, stocky men leaped upon him and disarmed him; another, quite tall, greeted him gravely:

"You are so kind. You have saved us a night and a day."

It was Red Scharlach. The men tied Lönnrot's hands. Lönnrot at last found his voice.

"Scharlach—*you* are looking for the secret Name?"

Scharlach stood there, impassive. He had not participated in the brief struggle, and now moved only to put out his hand for Lönnrot's revolver. But then he spoke, and Lönnrot heard in his voice a tired triumphance, a hatred as large as the universe, a sadness no smaller than that hatred.

"No," he said. "I am looking for something more fleeting and more perishable than that—I am looking for Erik Lönnrot. Three years ago, in a gambling den on the rue de Toulon, you arrested my brother and saw that he was sent to prison. My men rescued me from the shoot-out in a coupe, but not before I'd received a policeman's bullet in my gut. Nine days and nine nights I lay between life and death in this desolate symmetrical villa, consumed by fever, and that hateful two-faced Janus that looks toward the sunset and the dawn lent horror to my deliriums and my sleeplessness. I came to abominate my own body, I came to feel that two eyes, two hands, two lungs are as monstrous as two faces. An Irishman tried to convert me to belief in Christ; he would repeat, over and over, the goyim's saying: All roads lead to Rome. At night, my delirium would grow fat upon that metaphor: I sensed that the world was a labyrinth, impossible to escape—for all roads, even if they pretended to lead north or south, returned finally to Rome, which was also the rectangular prison where my brother lay dying, and which was also the Villa Triste-le-Roy. During those nights, I swore by the god that sees with two faces, and by all the gods of fever and of mirrors, to weave a labyrinth around the man who had imprisoned my brother. I have woven it, and it has stood firm: its materials are a dead heresiologue, a compass, an eighth-century cult, a Greek word, a dagger, the rhombuses of a paint factory. . . .

"The first term of the series was given me quite by chance. With some friends of mine—among them Daniel Azevedo—I had figured out a way to steal the tetrarch's sapphires. Azevedo, however, double-crossed us; he got drunk on the money we had advanced him and pulled the job a day early. But then he got lost in that huge hotel, and sometime around two o'clock in the morning he burst into Yarmolinsky's room. Yarmolinsky, who suffered from insomnia, was sitting at his typewriter typing. As coincidence would have it, he was making some notes, or writing an article perhaps, on the Name of God; he had just typed the words *The first letter of the Name has been written*. Azevedo told him to keep quiet; Yarmolinsky put out his hand toward the bell that would wake everyone in the hotel; Azevedo stabbed him once in the chest. The movement was almost reflexive; a half century of violence had taught him that the easiest and safest way is simply to kill. . . .Ten days later I learned from the *Yiddische Zeitung* that you were trying to find the key to Yarmolinsky's death among Yarmolinsky's writings. I read *A History of the Hasidim*; I learned that the reverent fear of speaking the Name of God had been the origin of the doctrine that that Name is omnipotent and occult. I learned that some Hasidim, in the quest for that secret Name, had gone so far as to commit human sacrifice. . . . I realized that you would conjecture that the Hasidim had sacrificed the rabbi; I set about justifying that conjecture.

"Marcelo Yarmolinsky died on the night of December third; I chose the third of January for the second 'sacrifice.' Yarmolinsky died in the north; for the second 'sacrifice,' the death should take place in the west. Daniel Azevedo was the necessary victim. He deserved to die; he was a man that acted on impulse and he was a traitor—if he were captured, he could destroy my plan. One of my men stabbed him; in order to link his body to the first one, I wrote *The second letter of the Name has been written* across the rhombuses of the paint factory.

"The third 'crime' was committed on the third of February. It was, as Treviranus guessed, a mere sham, a simulacrum. *I* am Gryphius-Ginzberg-Ginsburg; I spent one interminable week (supplemented by a tissue-thin false beard) in that perverse cubicle on the rue de Toulon, until my friends kidnapped me. Standing on the running board of the coupe, one of them scrawled on a pillar the words that you recall: *The last letter of the Name has been written.* That sentence revealed that this was a series of *three* crimes. At least that was how the man in the street interpreted it—but I had repeatedly dropped clues so that *you*, the *reasoning* Erik Lönnrot, would realize that there were actually *four.* One sign in the north, two more in the east and west, demand a fourth sign in the south—after all, the Tetragrammaton, the Name of God, YHVH, consists of *four* letters; the harlequins and the paint manufacturer's emblem suggest *four* terms. It was I who underlined that passage in Leusden's book. The passage says that Jews compute the day from sunset to sunset; the passage therefore gives one to understand that the deaths occurred on the *fourth* of each month. It was I who sent the equilateral triangle to Treviranus. I knew you would add the missing point, the point that makes a perfect rhombus, the point that fixes the place where a precise death awaits you. I have done all this, Erik Lönnrot, planned all this, in order to draw you to the solitudes of Triste-le-Roy."

Lönnrot avoided Scharlach's eyes. He looked at the trees and the sky subdivided into murky red, green, and yellow rhombuses. He felt a chill, and an impersonal, almost anonymous sadness. The night was dark now; from the dusty garden there rose the pointless cry of a bird. For the last time, Lönnrot considered the problem of the symmetrical, periodic murders.

"There are three lines too many in your labyrinth," he said at last. "I know of a Greek labyrinth that is but one straight line. So many philosophers have been lost upon that line that a mere detective might be pardoned if he became lost as well. When you hunt me down in another avatar of our lives, Scharlach, I suggest that you fake (or commit) one crime at A, a second crime at B, eight kilometers from A, then a third crime at C, four kilometers from A and B and halfway between them. Then wait for me at D, two kilometers from A and C, once again halfway between them. Kill me at D, as you are about to kill me at Triste-le-Roy."

"The next time I kill you," Scharlach replied, "I promise you the labyrinth that consists of a single straight line that is invisible and endless."

He stepped back a few steps. Then, very carefully, he fired.

1942

The Secret Miracle

And God caused him to die for an hundred years, and then
raised him to life. And God said, "How long hast thou
waited?" He said, "I have waited a day or part of a day."

Qur'ān, 2:261

On the night of March 14, 1939, in an apartment on Prague's
Zeltnergasse, Jaromir Hladik, author of the unfinished tragedy
The Enemies, a book titled *A Vindication of Eternity*, and a study of
Jakob Boehme's indirect Jewish sources, dreamed of a long game
of chess. The game was played not by two individuals, but by
two illustrious families; it had been started many centuries in the
past. No one could say what the forgotten prize was to be, but it
was rumored to be vast, perhaps even infinite. The chess pieces
and the chessboard themselves were in a secret tower. Jaromir (in
the dream) was the firstborn son of one of the contending families;
the clocks chimed the hour of the inescapable game; the dreamer
was running across the sand of a desert in the rain, but he could
recall neither the figures nor the rules of chess. At that point,
Hladik awoke. The din of the rain and the terrible clocks ceased.
A rhythmic and unanimous sound, punctuated by the barking of
orders, rose from the Zeltnergasse. It was sunrise, and the armored
vanguard of the Third Reich was rolling into Prague.

On the nineteenth, the authorities received a report from an
informer. That same day, toward dusk, Jaromir Hladik was
arrested. He was led to a white, aseptic jail on the opposite bank

of the Moldau. He was unable to refute even one of the Gestapo's charges: His mother's family's name was Jaroslavski, he came of Jewish blood, his article on Boehme dealt with a Jewish subject, his was one of the accusing signatures appended to a protest against the Anschluss. In 1928, he had translated the *Sefer Yetsirah* for Hermann Barsdorf Publishers; that company's effusive catalog had exaggerated (as commercial catalogs do) the translator's renown; the catalog had been perused by Capt. Julius Rothe, one of the officers in whose hands his fate now lay. There is no one who outside his own area of knowledge is not credulous; two or three adjectives in Fraktur were enough to persuade Julius Rothe of Hladik's preeminence, and therefore that he should be put to death—*pour encourager les autres*. The date was set for March 29, at 9:00 A.M.. That delay (whose importance the reader will soon discover) was caused by the administrative desire to work impersonally and deliberately, as vegetables do, or planets.

Hladik's first emotion was simple terror. He reflected that he wouldn't have quailed at being hanged, or decapitated, or having his throat slit, but being shot by a firing squad was unbearable. In vain he told himself a thousand times that the pure and universal act of dying was what ought to strike fear, not the concrete circumstances of it, and yet Hladik never wearied of picturing to himself those circumstances. Absurdly, he tried to foresee every variation. He anticipated the process endlessly, from the sleepless dawn to the mysterious discharge of the rifles. Long before the day that Julius Rothe had set, Hladik died hundreds of deaths— standing in courtyards whose shapes and angles ran the entire gamut of geometry, shot down by soldiers of changing faces and varying numbers who sometimes took aim at him from afar, sometimes from quite near. He faced his imaginary executions with true fear, perhaps with true courage. Each enactment lasted several seconds; when the circle was closed, Hladik would return, unendingly, to the shivering eve of his death. Then it occurred to him that reality seldom coincides with the way we envision it beforehand; he inferred, with perverse logic, that to foresee any particular detail is in fact to prevent its happening. Trusting in that frail magic, he began to invent horrible details—*so that they would not occur*; naturally he wound up fearing that those details might be prophetic. Miserable in the night, he tried to buttress his courage somehow on the fleeting stuff of time. He knew that time was rushing toward the morning of March 29; he reasoned aloud: *It is now the night of the twenty-second; so long as this night and six more last I am invulnerable, immortal.* He mused that the nights he slept were deep, dim cisterns into which he could sink. Sometimes, impatiently, he yearned for the shots that would end his life once and for all, the blast that would redeem him, for good or ill, from his vain imaginings. On the twenty-eighth, as the last rays of the sun were glimmering on the high bars of his window, he was diverted from those abject thoughts by the image of his play, *The Enemies.*

Hladik was past forty. Apart from a few friends and many routines, the problematic pursuit of literature constituted the whole of his life; like every writer, he measured other men's virtues by what they had accomplished, yet asked that other men measure him by what he planned someday to do. All the books he had sent to the press left him with complex regret. Into his articles on the work of Boehme, Ibn Ezra, and Fludd, he had poured mere diligence, application; into his translation of the *Sefer Yetsirah*, oversight, weariness, and conjecture. He judged *A Vindication of Eternity* to be less unsatisfactory, perhaps. The first volume documents the diverse eternities that mankind has invented, from Parmenides' static Being to Hinton's modifiable past; the second denies (with Francis Bradley) that all the events of the universe constitute a temporal series. It argues that the number of humankind's possible experiences is *not* infinite, and that a single "repetition" is sufficient to prove that time is a fallacy. . . .Unfortunately, no less fallacious are the arguments that prove that fallacy; Hladik was in the habit of ticking them off with a certain disdainful perplexity. He had also drafted a cycle of expressionist poems; these, to the poet's confusion, appeared in a 1924 anthology and there was never a subsequent anthology that didn't inherit them. With his verse drama *The Enemies*, Hladik believed he could redeem himself from all that equivocal and languid past. (He admired verse in drama because it does not allow the spectators to forget unreality, which is a condition of art.)

This play observed the unities of time, place, and action; it took place in Hradcany, in the library of Baron Römerstadt, on one of the last evenings of the nineteenth century. In Act I, Scene I, a stranger pays a visit to Römerstadt. (A clock strikes seven, a vehemence of last sunlight exalts the windowpanes, on a breeze float the ecstatic notes of a familiar Hungarian melody.) This visit is followed by others; the persons who come to importune Römerstadt are strangers to him, though he has the uneasy sense that he has seen them before, perhaps in a dream. All fawn upon him, but it is clear—first to the play's audience, then to the baron himself—that they are secret enemies, sworn to his destruction. Römerstadt manages to check or fend off their complex intrigues; in the dialogue they allude to his fiancée, Julia de Weidenau, and to one Jaroslav Kubin, who once importuned her with his love. Kubin has now gone mad, and believes himself to be Römerstadt. . . .The dangers mount; by the end of the second act, Römerstadt finds himself forced to kill one of the conspirators. Then the third and last act begins. Little by little, incoherences multiply; actors come back onstage who had apparently been discarded from the plot; for one instant, the man that Römerstadt killed returns. Someone points out that the hour has grown no later: the clock strikes seven; upon the high windowpanes the western sunlight shimmers; the thrilling Hungarian melody floats upon the air. The first interlocutor comes onstage again and repeats the same words he spoke in Act I, Scene I. Without the least surprise or astonishment, Römerstadt talks with him; the audience realizes that Römerstadt is the pitiable Jaroslav Kubin. The play has not taken place; it is the circular delirium that Kubin endlessly experiences and reexperiences.

Hladik had never asked himself whether this tragicomedy of errors was banal or admirable, carefully plotted or accidental. In the design I have outlined here, he had intuitively hit upon the best way of hiding his shortcomings and giving full play to his strengths, the possibility of rescuing (albeit symbolically) that which was fundamental to his life. He had finished the first act and one or another scene of the third; the metrical nature of the play allowed him to go over it continually, correcting the hexameters, without a manuscript. It occurred to him that he still had two acts to go, yet very soon he was to die. In the darkness he spoke with God. *If,* he prayed, *I do somehow exist, if I am not one of Thy repetitions or errata, then I exist as the author of* The Enemies. *In order to complete that play, which can justify me and justify Thee as well, I need one more year. Grant me those days, Thou who art the centuries and time itself.* It was the last night, the most monstrous night, but ten minutes later sleep flooded Hladik like some dark ocean.

Toward dawn, he dreamed that he was in hiding, in one of the naves of the Clementine Library. *What are you looking for?* a librarian wearing dark glasses asked him. *I'm looking for God,* Hladik replied. *God,* the librarian said, *is in one of the letters on one of the pages of one of the four hundred thousand volumes in the Clementine. My parents and my parents' parents searched for that letter; I myself have gone blind searching for it.* He removed his spectacles and Hladik saw his eyes, which were dead. A reader came in to return an atlas. *This atlas is worthless,* he said, and handed it to Hladik. Hladik opened it at random. He saw a map of India—a dizzying page. Suddenly certain, he touched one of the tiny letters. A voice that was everywhere spoke to him: *The time for your labor has been granted.* Here Hladik awoke.

He remembered that the dreams of men belong to God and

that Maimonides had written that the words of a dream, when they are clear and distinct and one cannot see who spoke them, are holy. Hladik put his clothes on; two soldiers entered the cell and ordered him to follow them.

From inside his cell, Hladik had thought that when he emerged he would see a maze of galleries, stairways, and wings. Reality was not so rich; he and the soldiers made their way down a single iron staircase into a rear yard. Several soldiers—some with their uniforms unbuttoned—were looking over a motorcycle, arguing about it. The sergeant looked at his watch; it was eight forty-four. They had to wait until nine. Hladik, feeling more insignificant than ill fortuned, sat down on a pile of firewood. He noticed that the soldiers' eyes avoided his own. To make the wait easier, the sergeant handed him a cigarette. Hladik did not smoke; he accepted the cigarette out of courtesy, or out of humility. When he lighted it, he saw that his hands were trembling. The day clouded over; the soldiers were speaking in low voices, as though he were already dead. Vainly he tried to recall the woman that Julia de Weidenau had symbolized. . . .

The firing squad fell in, lined up straight. Hladik, standing against the prison wall, awaited the discharge. Someone was afraid the wall would be spattered with blood; the prisoner was ordered to come forward a few steps. Absurdly, Hladik was reminded of the preliminary shufflings-about of photographers. A heavy drop of rain grazed Hladik's temple and rolled slowly down his cheek; the sergeant called out the final order.

The physical universe stopped.

The weapons converged upon Hladik, but the men who were to kill him were immobile. The sergeant's arm seemed to freeze, eternal, in an inconclusive gesture. On one of the paving stones of the yard, a bee cast a motionless shadow. As though in a painting, the wind had died. Hladik attempted a scream, a syllable, the twisting of a hand. He realized that he was paralyzed. He could hear not the slightest murmur of the halted world. *I am in hell*, he thought, *I am dead*. Then *I am mad*, he thought. And then, *time has halted*. Then he reflected that if that were true, his thoughts would have halted as well. He tried to test this conjecture: he repeated (without moving his lips) Virgil's mysterious fourth eclogue. He imagined that the now-remote soldiers must be as disturbed by this as he was; he wished he could communicate with them. He was surprised and puzzled to feel neither the slightest weariness nor any faintness from his long immobility. After an indeterminate time, he slept. When he awoke, the world was still motionless and muffled. The drop of water still hung on his cheek; on the yard, there still hung the shadow of the bee; in the air the smoke from the cigarette he'd smoked had never wafted away. Another of those "days" passed before Hladik understood.

He had asked God for an entire year in which to finish his work; God in His omnipotence had granted him a year. God had performed for him a secret miracle: the German bullet would kill him, at the determined hour, but in Hladik's mind a year would pass between the order to fire and the discharge of the rifles. From perplexity Hladik moved to stupor, from stupor to resignation, from resignation to sudden gratitude.

He had no document but his memory; the fact that he had to learn each hexameter as he added it imposed upon him a providential strictness, unsuspected by those who essay and then forget vague provisional paragraphs. He did not work for posterity, nor did he work for God, whose literary preferences were largely unknown to him. Painstakingly, motionlessly, secretly, he forged in time his grand invisible labyrinth. He redid the third act twice. He struck out one and another overly obvious symbol—the repeated chimings of the clock, the music. No detail was irksome to him. He cut, condensed, expanded; in some cases he decided the original version should stand. He came to love the courtyard, the prison; one of the faces that stood before him altered his conception of Römerstadt's character. He discovered that the

hard-won cacophonies that were so alarming to Flaubert are mere
visual superstitions—weaknesses and irritations of the written,
not the sounded, word. . . .He completed his play; only a single
epithet was left to be decided upon now. He found it; the drop of
water rolled down his cheek. He began a maddened cry, he shook
his head, and the fourfold volley felled him.

Jaromir Hladik died on the twenty-ninth of March, at 9:02
A.M..

1943

Three Versions of Judas

There seemed a certainty in degradation.
T. E. Lawrence, *The Seven Pillars of Wisdom*, CIII

In Asia Minor or in Alexandria, in the second century of our faith, in the days when Basilides proclaimed that the cosmos was a reckless or maleficent improvisation by angels lacking in perfection, Nils Runeberg, with singular intellectual passion, would have led one of the gnostic conventicles. Dante might have consigned him to a sepulcher of fire; his name would have helped swell the catalogs of minor heresiarchs, between Satornilus and Carpocrates; one or another fragment of his teachings, bedizened with invective, would have been recorded for posterity in the apocryphal *Liber adversus omnes hæreses* or would have perished when the burning of a monastery's library devoured the last copy of the *Syntagma*. Instead, God allotted him the twentieth century and the university city of Lund. There, in 1904, he published the first edition of *Kristus och Judas*; there, in 1909, his magnum opus, *Den hemlige Frälsaren*. (Of this last-named book there is a German version, translated in 1912 by Emil Schering; it is titled *Der heimliche Heiland*.)

Before undertaking an examination of the works mentioned above, it is important to reiterate that Nils Runeberg, a member of the National Evangelical Union, was a deeply religious man. At a *soirée* in Paris or even in Buenos Aires, a man of letters might very well rediscover Runeberg's theses; those theses, proposed at such a *soirée*, would be slight and pointless exercises in slovenliness or blasphemy. For Runeberg, they were the key that unlocked one of theology's central mysteries; they were the stuff of study and meditation, of historical and philological controversy, of arrogance, of exultation, and of terror. They justified and destroyed his life. Those who peruse this article should likewise consider that it records only Runeberg's conclusions, not his dialectic or his proofs. It will be said that the conclusion no doubt preceded its "proofs." But what man can content himself with seeking out proofs for a thing that not even he himself believes in, or whose teaching he cares naught for?

The first edition of *Kristus och Judas* bears this categorical epigraph, whose meaning, years afterward, Nils Runeberg himself was monstrously to expatiate upon: *It is not one thing, but all the things which legend attributes to Judas Iscariot that are false* (de Quincey, 1857). Like a certain German before him, de Quincey speculated that Judas had delivered up Christ in order to force Him to declare His divinity and set in motion a vast uprising against Rome's yoke; Runeberg suggests a vindication of a *metaphysical* nature. Cleverly, he begins by emphasizing how superfluous Judas' action was. He observes (as Robertson had) that in order to identify a teacher who preached every day in the synagogue and worked miracles in the plain sight of thousands of people, there was no need of betrayal by one of the teacher's own apostles. That is precisely, however, what occurred. To assume an error in the Scriptures is intolerable, but it is no less intolerable to assume that a random act intruded into the most precious event in the history of the world. *Ergo*, Judas' betrayal was not a random act, but predetermined, with its own mysterious place in the economy of redemption. Runeberg continues: The Word, when it was made Flesh, passed from omnipresence into space, from eternity into history, from unlimited joy and happiness into mutability and death; to repay that sacrifice, it was needful that a man (in representation of all mankind) make a sacrifice of equal worth.

Judas Iscariot was that man. Alone among the apostles, Judas sensed Jesus' secret divinity and His terrible purpose. The Word had stooped to become mortal; Judas, a disciple of the Word, would stoop to become an informer (the most heinous crime that infamy will bear) and to dwell amid inextinguishable flames. As below, so above; the forms of earth correspond to the forms of heaven; the blotches of the skin are a map of the incorruptible constellations; Judas is somehow a reflection of Jesus. From that conclusion derive the thirty pieces of silver and the kiss; from that conclusion derives the voluntary death, so as even more emphatically to merit reprobation. Thus did Nils Runeberg explain the enigma that is Judas.

Theologians of every faith brought forth refutations. Lars Peter Engström accused Runeberg of ignoring the hypostatic union; Axel Borelius, of rekindling the Docetic heresy, which denied Jesus' humanity; the steely bishop of Lund accused him of contradicting Chapter 22, verse 3 of the Gospel According to St. Luke.

These diverse anathemas did have their influence on Runeberg, who partially rewrote the reprehended book and modified its doctrine. He abandoned the theological ground to his adversaries and proposed oblique arguments of a moral order. He admitted that Jesus, "who could call upon the considerable resources that Omnipotence can offer," had no need of a man to carry out His plan for the redemption of all mankind. Then he rebutted those who claimed that we know nothing of the inexplicable betrayer. We know, Runeberg said, that he was one of the apostles, one of those chosen to herald the kingdom of heaven, to heal the sick, cleanse the lepers, raise the dead, and cast out demons (Matthew 10:7–8, Luke 9:1). The acts of a man thus singled out by the Redeemer merit the most sympathetic interpretation we can give them. To impute his crime to greed (as some have done, citing John 12:6) is to settle for the basest motive. Nils Runeberg proposed a motive at the opposite extreme: a hyperbolic, even limitless asceticism. The ascetic, *ad majorem Dei gloriam*, debases and mortifies the flesh; Judas debased and mortified the spirit. He renounced honor, goodness, peace, the kingdom of heaven, as others, less heroically, renounce pleasure.[1] He plotted his sins with terrible lucidity. In adultery, tenderness and abnegation often play a role; in homicide, courage; in blasphemy and profanation, a certain satanic zeal. Judas chose sins unvisited by any virtue: abuse of confidence (John 12:6) and betrayal. He labored with titanic humility; he believed himself unworthy of being good. Paul wrote: *He that glorieth, let him glory in the Lord* (I Corinthians 1:31); Judas sought hell because joy in the Lord was enough for him. He thought that happiness, like goodness, is a divine attribute, which should not be usurped by men.[2]

Many have discovered, after the fact, that in Runeberg's justifiable beginnings lies his extravagant end, and that *Den hemlige Frälsaren* is a mere perversion or exasperation of his *Kristus och Judas*. In late 1907, Runeberg completed and revised the manuscript text; almost two years passed before he delivered it to the publisher. In October, 1909, the book appeared with a foreword (lukewarm to the point of being enigmatic) by the Danish Hebrew scholar Erik Erfjord, and with the following epigraph: *He was in the world, and the world was made by him, and the world knew him not* (John 1:10). The book's general argument is not complex, although its conclusion is monstrous. God, argues Nils Runeberg, stooped to become man for the redemption of the human race;

---

1. Borelius sarcastically asks: *Why did he not renounce renunciation? Why not renounce the renunciation of renunciation?*

2. In a book unknown to Runeberg, Euclides da Cunha* notes that in the view of the Canudos heresiarch Antonio Conselheiro,* virtue "is a near impiety." The Argentine reader will recall analogous passages in the work of the poet Almafuerte.* In the symbolist journal *Sju insegel*, Runeberg published an assiduous descriptive poem titled "The Secret Lake"; the first verses narrate the events of a tumultuous day, while the last record the discovery of a glacial "tarn." The poet suggests that the eternity of those silent waters puts right our useless violence and—somehow—both allows it and absolves it. The poem ends with these words: "The water of the forest is happy; we can be evil and in pain."

we might well then presume that the sacrifice effected by Him was perfect, not invalidated or attenuated by omissions. To limit His suffering to the agony of one afternoon on the cross is blasphemous.[1] To claim that He was man, and yet was incapable of sin, is to fall into contradiction; the attributes *impeccabilitas* and *humanitas* are incompatible. Kemnitz will allow that the Redeemer could feel weariness, cold, distress, hunger, and thirst; one might also allow Him to be able to sin and be condemned to damnation. For many, the famous words in Isaiah 53:2–3, *He shall grow up before him as a tender plant, and as a root out of a dry ground: he hath no form nor comeliness; and when we shall see him, there is no beauty that we should desire him. He is despised and rejected of men; a man of sorrows, and acquainted with grief,* are a foreshadowing of the Crucified Christ at the hour of His death. For some (Hans Lassen Martensen, for example), they are a refutation of the loveliness that the vulgar consensus attributes to Christ; for Runeberg, they are the detailed prophecy not of a moment but of the entire horrendous future, in Time and in Eternity, of the Word made Flesh. God was made totally man, but man to the point of iniquity, man to the point of reprobation and the Abyss. In order to save us, He could have chosen *any* of the lives that weave the confused web of history: He could have been Alexander or Pythagoras or Rurik or Jesus; he chose an abject existence: He was Judas.

In vain did the bookstores of Stockholm and Lund offer readers

1. Maurice Abramowicz observes: "Jésus, d'après ce scandinave, a toujours le beau rôle; ses déboires, grâce à la science des typographes, jouissent d'une réputation polyglotte; sa résidence de trente-trois ans parmi les humains ne fut, en somme, qu'une villégiature." In Appendix III to his *Christelige Dogmatik*, Erfjord rebuts this passage. He notes that the crucifixion of God has not ended, because that which happened once in time is repeated endlessly in eternity. Judas, *now*, continues to hold out his hand for the silver, continues to kiss Jesus' cheek, continues to scatter the pieces of silver in the temple, continues to knot the noose on the field of blood. (In order to justify this statement, Erfjord cites the last chapter of the first volume of Jaromir Hladik's *Vindication of Eternity*.)

this revelation. The incredulous considered it, *a priori*, a vapid and tedious theological game; theologians disdained it. Runeberg sensed in that ecumenical indifference an almost miraculous confirmation. God had ordered that indifference; God did not want His terrible secret spread throughout the earth. Runeberg realized that the hour was not yet come. He felt that ancient, divine curses were met in him. He recalled Elijah and Moses, who covered their faces upon the mountain so as not to look upon God; Isaiah, who was terrified when his eyes beheld the One whose glory fills the earth; Saul, whose eyes were blinded on the road to Damascus; the rabbi Simeon ben Azai, who saw the Garden and died; the famous wizard John of Viterbo, who went mad when the Trinity was revealed to him; the Midrashim, who abominate those who speak the *Shem Hamephorash*, the Secret Name of God. Was it not that dark sin that he, Runeberg, was guilty of? Might not that be the blasphemy against the Holy Ghost (Matthew 12:31) which shall not be forgiven? Valerius Soranus died for revealing the hidden name of Rome; what infinite punishment would be Runeberg's for having discovered and revealed the terrible name of God?

Drunk with sleeplessness and his dizzying dialectic, Nils Runeberg wandered the streets of Mälmo, crying out for a blessing—that he be allowed to share the Inferno with the Redeemer.

He died of a ruptured aneurysm on March 1, 1912. Heresiologists will perhaps remember him; he added to the concept of the Son, which might have been thought long spent, the complexities of misery and evil.

1944

The End

Lying on his back, Recabarren opened his eyes a bit and saw the sloping ceiling of thick cane. From the other room there came the strumming of a guitar, like some inconsequential labyrinth, infinitely tangling and untangling. . . .Little by little, reality came back to him, the ordinary things that now would always be just *these* ordinary things. He looked down without pity at his great useless body, the plain wool poncho that wrapped his legs. Outside, beyond the thick bars at his window, spread the flatland and the evening; he had slept, but the sky was still filled with light. He groped with his left arm until he found the brass cowbell that hung at the foot of the cot. He shook it once or twice; outside his door, the unassuming chords continued.

The guitar was being played by a black man who had shown up one night flattering himself that he was a singer; he had challenged another stranger to a song contest, the way traveling singers did. Beaten, he went on showing up at the general-store-and-bar night after night, as though he were waiting for someone. He spent hours with the guitar, but he never sang again; it could be that the defeat had turned him bitter. People had grown used to the inoffensive man. Recabarren, the owner of the bar, would never forget that contest; the next day, as he was trying to straighten some bales of *yerba*, his right side had suddenly gone dead on him, and he discovered that he couldn't talk. From learning to pity the misfortunes of the heroes of our novels, we wind up feeling too much pity for our own; but not Recabarren,

138

who accepted his paralysis as he had earlier accepted the severity and the solitudes of the Americas. A man in the habit of living in the present, as animals do, he now looked up at the sky and reflected that the red ring around the moon was a sign of rain.

A boy with Indian-like features (Recabarren's son, perhaps) opened the door a crack. Recabarren asked him with his eyes whether anybody was around; the boy, not one to talk much, made a motion with his hand to say there wasn't—the black man didn't count. Then the prostrate man was left alone; his left hand played awhile with the bell, as though exercising some power.

The plains, in the last rays of the sun, were almost abstract, as though seen in a dream. A dot wavered on the horizon, then grew until it became a horseman riding, or so it seemed, toward the house. Recabarren could make out the broad-brimmed hat, the dark poncho, the piebald horse, but not the face of the rider, who finally reined in the horse and came toward the house at an easy trot. Some two hundred yards out, he veered off to the side. At that, the man was out of Recabarren's line of sight, but Recabarren heard him speak, get down off his horse, tie it to the post, and with a firm step enter the bar.

Without raising his eyes from the guitar, where he seemed to be looking for something, the black man spoke.

"I *knew* I could count on you, sir," he softly said.

"And I knew I could count on you, old nigger," the other man replied, his voice harsh. "A heap of days I've made you wait, but here I am."

There was a silence. Then the black man spoke again.

"I'm getting used to waiting. I've been waiting now for seven years."

Unhurried, the other man explained:

"It'd been longer than seven years that I'd gone without seeing my children. I found them that day, and I wouldn't have it so's I looked to them like a man on his way to a knife fight."*

"I understood that," the black man said. "I hope they were all in good health."

The stranger, who had sat down at the bar, gave a hearty laugh at that. He ordered a drink and took a sip or two, but didn't finish it.

"I gave them some advice," he said, "which is something you can never get too much of and doesn't cost a lot. I told them, among other things, that a man ought not to go spilling another man's blood."

A slow chord preceded the black man's response:

"Good advice, too. That way they won't grow up to be like us."

"Not like me, anyway," said the stranger, who then added, as though thinking out loud: "Fate would have it that I kill, and now it's put a knife in my hand again."

"Fall's coming on," the black man observed, as though he hadn't heard, "and the days are getting shorter."

"The light that's left will be enough for me," replied the other man, getting to his feet.

He stood square before the black man and in a tired voice said to him, "Leave that guitar alone, now—you've got another kind of contest to try to win today."

The two men walked toward the door. As the black man stepped outside, he murmured, "Could be this one goes as bad f'r me as the other one did."

"It's not that the first one went bad for you," the other man answered, serious. "It's that you couldn't hardly wait to get to the second one."

They walked beside each other until they got some distance from the houses. One place on the plains was much like another, and the moon was bright. Suddenly they looked at each other, stopped, and the stranger took off his spurs. They already had their ponchos wrapped around their forearms when the black man spoke.

"One thing I want to ask you before we get down to it. I want you to put all your courage and all your skill into this, like you did seven years ago when you killed my brother."

For perhaps the first time in their exchange, Martín Fierro heard the hatred. His blood felt it, like a sharp prod. They circled, clashed, and sharp steel marked the black man's face.

There is an hour just at evening when the plains seem on the verge of saying something; they never do, or perhaps they do—eternally—though we don't understand it, or perhaps we do understand but what they say is as untranslatable as music. . . .From his cot, Recabarren saw the end. A thrust, and the black man dodged back, lost his footing, feigned a slash to his opponent's face, and then lunged out with a deep jab that buried the knife in his belly. Then came another thrust, which the storekeeper couldn't see, and Fierro did not get up. Unmoving, the black man seemed to stand watch over the agonizing death. He wiped off the bloody knife in the grass and walked slowly back toward the houses, never looking back. His work of vengeance done, he was nobody now. Or rather, he was the other one: there was neither destination nor destiny on earth for him, and he had killed a man.

The Cult of the Phoenix

Those who write that the cult of the Phoenix had its origin in Heliopolis, and claim that it derives from the religious restoration that followed the death of the reformer Amenhotep IV, cite the writings of Herodotus and Tacitus and the inscriptions on Egyptian monuments, but they are unaware, perhaps willfully unaware, that the cult's designation as "the cult of the Phoenix" can be traced back no farther than to Hrabanus Maurus and that the earliest sources (the *Saturnalia*, say, or Flavius Josephus) speak only of "the People of the Practice" or "the People of the Secret." In the conventicles of Ferrara, Gregorovius observed that mention of the Phoenix was very rare in the spoken language; in Geneva, I have had conversations with artisans who did not understand me when I asked whether they were men of the Phoenix but immediately admitted to being men of the Secret. Unless I am mistaken, much the same might be said about Buddhists: The name by which the world knows them is not the name that they themselves pronounce.

On one altogether too famous page, Moklosich has equated the members of the cult of the Phoenix with the gypsies. In Chile and in Hungary, there are both gypsies and members of the sect; apart from their ubiquity, the two groups have very little in common. Gypsies are horse traders, pot-makers, blacksmiths, and fortune-tellers; the members of the cult of the Phoenix are generally contented practitioners of the "liberal professions." Gypsies are of a certain physical type, and speak, or used to speak, a secret language; the members of the cult are indistinguishable from other men, and the proof of this is that they have never been persecuted. Gypsies are picturesque, and often inspire bad poets; ballads, photographs, and boleros fail to mention the members of the cult. . . .Martin Buber says that Jews are essentially sufferers; not all the members of the cult are, and some actively abhor pathos. That public and well-known truth suffices to refute the vulgar error (absurdly defended by Urmann) which sees the roots of the Phoenix as lying in Israel. People's reasoning goes more or less this way: Urmann was a sensitive man; Urmann was a Jew; Urmann made a habit of visiting the members of the cult in the Jewish ghettos of Prague; the affinity that Urmann sensed proves a real relationship. In all honesty, I cannot concur with that conclusion. That the members of the cult should, in a Jewish milieu, resemble Jews proves nothing; what cannot be denied is that they, like Hazlitt's infinite Shakespeare, resemble every man in the world. They are all things to all men, like the Apostle; a few days ago, Dr. Juan Francisco Amaro, of Paysandú, pondered the ease with which they assimilate, the ease with which they "naturalize" themselves.

I have said that the history of the cult records no persecutions. That is true, but since there is no group of human beings that does not include adherents of the sect of the Phoenix, it is also true that there has been no persecution or severity that the members of the cult have not suffered *and carried out.* In the wars of the Western world and in the distant wars of Asia, their blood has been spilled for centuries, under enemy flags; it is hardly worth their while to identify themselves with every nation on the globe.

Lacking a sacred book to unite them as the Scriptures unite Israel, lacking a common memory, lacking that other memory that is a common language, scattered across the face of the earth, diverse in color and in feature, there is but one thing—the Secret—that unites them, and that *will* unite them until the end of time. Once, in addition to the Secret there was a legend (and perhaps a cosmogonic myth), but the superficial men of the Phoenix have forgotten it, and today all that is left to them is the dim and obscure story of a punishment. A punishment, or a pact, or a privilege—versions differ; but what one may dimly see in all of them is the judgment of a God who promises eternity to a race of beings if its men, generation upon generation, perform a certain ritual. I have compared travelers' reports, I have spoken with patriarchs and theologians; I can attest that the performance of that ritual is the only religious practice observed by the members of the cult. The ritual is, in fact, the Secret. The Secret, as I have said, is transmitted from generation to generation, but tradition forbids a mother from teaching it to her children, as it forbids priests from doing so; initiation into the mystery is the task of the lowest individuals of the group. A slave, a leper, or a beggar plays the role of mystagogue. A child, too, may catechize another child. The act itself is trivial, the matter of a moment's time, and it needs no description. The materials used are cork, wax, or gum arabic. (In the liturgy there is mention of "slime"; pond slime is often used as well.) There are no temples dedicated expressly to the cult's worship, but ruins, cellars, or entryways are considered appropriate sites. The Secret is sacred, but that does not prevent its being a bit ridiculous; the performance of it is furtive, even clandestine, and its adepts do not speak of it. There are no decent words by which to call it, but it is understood that all words somehow name it, or rather, that they inevitably allude to it— and so I have said some insignificant thing in conversation and have seen adepts smile or grow uncomfortable because they sensed I had touched upon the Secret. In Germanic literatures there are poems written by members of the cult whose nominal subject is the sea or twilight; more than once I have heard people say that these poems are, somehow, symbols of the Secret. *Orbis terrarum est speculum Ludi*, goes an apocryphal saying reported by du Cange in his Glossary. A kind of sacred horror keeps some of the faithful from performing that simplest of rituals; they are despised by the other members of the sect, but they despise themselves even more. Those, on the other hand, who deliberately renounce the Practice and achieve direct commerce with the Deity command great respect; such men speak of that commerce using figures from the liturgy, and so we find that John of the Rood wrote as follows:

> *Let the Nine Firmaments be told*
> *That God is delightful as the Cork and Mire.*

On three continents I have merited the friendship of many worshipers of the Phoenix; I know that the Secret at first struck them as banal, shameful, vulgar, and (stranger still) unbelievable. They could not bring themselves to admit that their parents had ever stooped to such acts. It is odd that the Secret did not die out long ago; but in spite of the world's vicissitudes, in spite of wars and exoduses, it does, in its full awesomeness, come to all the faithful. Someone has even dared to claim that by now it is instinctive.

The South

The man that stepped off the boat in Buenos Aires in 1871 was a minister of the Evangelical Church; his name was Johannes Dahlmann. By 1939, one of his grandsons, Juan Dahlmann, was secretary of a municipal library on Calle Córdoba and considered himself profoundly Argentine. His maternal grandfather had been Francisco Flores, of the 2nd Infantry of the Line, who died on the border of Buenos Aires* from a spear wielded by the Indians under Catriel.* In the contrary pulls from his two lineages, Juan Dahlmann (perhaps impelled by his Germanic blood) chose that of his romantic ancestor, or that of a romantic death. That slightly willful but never ostentatious "Argentinization" drew sustenance from an old sword, a locket containing the daguerreotype of a bearded, inexpressive man, the joy and courage of certain melodies, the habit of certain verses in *Martín Fierro*, the passing years, a certain lack of spiritedness, and solitude. At the price of some self-denial, Dahlmann had managed to save the shell of a large country house in the South that had once belonged to the Flores family; one of the touchstones of his memory was the image of the eucalyptus trees and the long pink-colored house that had once been scarlet. His work, and perhaps his indolence, held him in the city. Summer after summer he contented himself with the abstract idea of possession and with the certainty that his house was waiting for him, at a precise place on the flatlands. In late February, 1939, something happened to him.

Though blind to guilt, fate can be merciless with the slightest distractions. That afternoon Dahlmann had come upon a copy (from which some pages were missing) of Weil's *Arabian Nights*; eager to examine his find, he did not wait for the elevator—he hurriedly took the stairs. Something in the dimness brushed his forehead—a bat? a bird? On the face of the woman who opened the door to him, he saw an expression of horror, and the hand he passed over his forehead came back red with blood. His brow had caught the edge of a recently painted casement window that somebody had forgotten to close. Dahlmann managed to sleep, but by the early hours of morning he was awake, and from that time on, the flavor of all things was monstrous to him. Fever wore him away, and illustrations from the *Arabian Nights* began to illuminate nightmares. Friends and members of his family would visit him and with exaggerated smiles tell him how well he looked. Dahlmann, in a kind of feeble stupor, would hear their words, and it would amaze him that they couldn't see he was in hell. Eight days passed, like eight hundred years. One afternoon, his usual physician appeared with a new man, and they drove Dahlmann to a sanatorium on Calle Ecuador; he needed to have an X ray. Sitting in the cab they had hired to drive them, Dahlmann reflected that he might, at last, in a room that was not his own, be able to sleep. He felt happy, he felt like talking, but the moment they arrived, his clothes were stripped from him, his head was shaved, he was strapped with metal bands to a table, he was blinded and dizzied with bright lights, his heart and lungs were listened to, and a man in a surgical mask stuck a needle in his arm. He awoke nauseated, bandaged, in a cell much like the bottom of a well, and in the days and nights that followed, he realized that until then he had been only somewhere on the outskirts of hell. Ice left but the slightest trace of coolness in his mouth. During these days, Dahlmann hated every inch of himself; he hated his identity, his bodily needs, his humiliation, the beard that prickled his face. He stoically suffered the treatments administered to him, which were quite painful, but when the surgeon told him he'd been on the verge of death from septicemia, Dahlmann, suddenly self-pitying, broke down and cried. The physical miseries, the unending anticipation of bad nights had not allowed him to think about anything as abstract as death. The next day, the surgeon told him he was coming right along, and that he'd soon be able to go out to the country house to convalesce. Incredibly, the promised day arrived.

Reality is partial to symmetries and slight anachronisms; Dahlmann had come to the sanatorium in a cab, and it was a cab that took him to the station at Plaza Constitución. The first cool breath of autumn, after the oppression of the summer, was like a natural symbol of his life brought back from fever and the brink of death. The city, at that seven o'clock in the morning, had not lost that look of a ramshackle old house that cities take on at night; the streets were like long porches and corridors, the plazas like interior courtyards. After his long stay in hospital, Dahlmann took it all in with delight and a touch of vertigo; a few seconds before his eyes registered them, he would recall the corners, the marquees, the modest variety of Buenos Aires. In the yellow light of the new day, it all came back to him.

Everyone knows that the South begins on the other side of Avenida Rivadavia. Dahlmann had often said that that was no mere saying, that by crossing Rivadavia one entered an older and more stable world. From the cab, he sought among the new buildings the window barred with wrought iron, the door knocker, the arch of a doorway, the long entryway, the almost-secret courtyard.

In the grand hall of the station he saw that he had thirty minutes before his train left. He suddenly remembered that there was a café on Calle Brasil (a few yards from Yrigoyen's house) where there was a huge cat that would let people pet it, like some disdainful deity. He went in. There was the cat, asleep. He ordered a cup of coffee, slowly spooned sugar into it, tasted it (a pleasure that had been forbidden him in the clinic), and thought, while he stroked the cat's black fur, that this contact was illusory, that he and the cat were separated as though by a pane of glass, because man lives in time, in successiveness, while the magical animal lives in the present, in the eternity of the instant.

The train, stretching along the next-to-last platform, was waiting. Dahlmann walked through the cars until he came to one that was almost empty. He lifted his bag onto the luggage rack; when the train pulled out, he opened his bag and after a slight hesitation took from it the first volume of *The Arabian Nights*. To travel with this book so closely linked to the history of his torment was an affirmation that the torment was past, and was a joyous, secret challenge to the frustrated forces of evil.

On both sides of the train, the city unraveled into suburbs; that sight, and later the sight of lawns and large country homes, led Dahlmann to put aside his reading. The truth is, Dahlmann read very little; the lodestone mountain and the genie sworn to kill the man who released him from the bottle were, as anyone will admit, wondrous things, but not much more wondrous than this morning and the fact of being. Happiness distracted him from Scheherazade and her superfluous miracles; Dahlmann closed the book and allowed himself simply to live.

Lunch (with bouillon served in bowls of shining metal, as in the now-distant summers of his childhood) was another quiet, savored pleasure.

Tomorrow I will wake up at my ranch, he thought, and it was as though he were two men at once: the man gliding along through the autumn day and the geography of his native land, and the other man, imprisoned in a sanatorium and subjected to methodical attentions. He saw unplastered brick houses, long and angular, infinitely watching the trains go by; he saw horsemen on the clod-strewn roads; he saw ditches and lakes and pastures; he saw long glowing clouds that seemed made of marble, and all these things were fortuitous, like some dream of the flat prairies. He also thought he recognized trees and crops that he couldn't have told one the name of—his direct knowledge of the country was considerably inferior to his nostalgic, literary knowledge.

From time to time he nodded off, and in his dreams there was the rushing momentum of the train. Now the unbearable white sun of midday was the yellow sun that comes before nightfall and that soon would turn to red. The car was different now, too; it was not the same car that had pulled out of the station in Buenos Aires—the plains and the hours had penetrated and transfigured it. Outside, the moving shadow of the train stretched out toward the horizon. The elemental earth was not disturbed by settlements or any other signs of humanity. All was vast, but at the same time intimate and somehow secret. In all the immense countryside, there would sometimes be nothing but a bull. The solitude was perfect, if perhaps hostile, and Dahlmann almost suspected that he was traveling not only into the South but into the past. From that fantastic conjecture he was distracted by the conductor, who seeing Dahlmann's ticket informed him that the train would not be leaving him at the usual station, but at a different one, a little before it, that Dahlmann barely knew. (The man added an explanation that Dahlmann didn't try to understand, didn't even listen to, because the mechanics of it didn't matter.)

The train came to its laborious halt in virtually the middle of the countryside. The station sat on the other side of the tracks, and was hardly more than a covered platform. They had no vehicle there, but the station-master figured Dahlmann might be able to find one at a store he directed him to—ten or twelve blocks away.

Dahlmann accepted the walk as a small adventure. The sun had sunk below the horizon now, but one final splendor brought a glory to the living yet silent plains before they were blotted out by night. Less to keep from tiring himself than to make those things last, Dahlmann walked slowly, inhaling with grave happiness the smell of clover.

The store had once been bright red, but the years had tempered its violent color (to its advantage). There was something in its sorry architecture that reminded Dahlmann of a steel engraving, perhaps from an old edition of *Paul et Virginie*. There were several horses tied to the rail in front. Inside, Dahlmann thought he recognized the owner; then he realized that he'd been fooled by the man's resemblance to one of the employees at the sanatorium. When the man heard Dahlmann's story, he said he'd have the calash harnessed up; to add yet another event to that day, and to pass the time, Dahlmann decided to eat there in the country store.

At one table some rough-looking young men were noisily eating and drinking; at first Dahlmann didn't pay much attention. On the floor, curled against the bar, lay an old man, as motionless as an object. The many years had worn him away and polished him, as a stone is worn smooth by running water or a saying is polished by generations of humankind. He was small, dark, and dried up, and he seemed to be outside time, in a sort of eternity. Dahlmann was warmed by the rightness of the man's hairband, the baize poncho he wore, his gaucho trousers,* and the boots made out of the skin of a horse's leg, and he said to himself, recalling futile arguments with people from districts in the North, or from Entre Ríos, that only in the South did gauchos like that exist anymore.

Dahlmann made himself comfortable near the window. Little by little, darkness was enveloping the countryside, but the smells and sounds of the plains still floated in through the thick iron grate at the window. The storekeeper brought him sardines and then roast meat; Dahlmann washed them down with more than one glass of red wine. Idly, he savored the harsh bouquet of the wine and let his gaze wander over the store, which by now had turned a little sleepy. The kerosene lantern hung from one of the beams. There were three customers at the other table: two looked like laborers; the other, with coarse, Indian-like features, sat drinking with his wide-brimmed hat on. Dahlmann suddenly felt something lightly brush his face. Next to the tumbler of cloudy glass, on one of the stripes in the tablecloth, lay a little ball of wadded bread. That was all, but somebody had thrown it at him.

The drinkers at the other table seemed unaware of his presence. Dahlmann, puzzled, decided that nothing had happened, and he opened the volume of *The Arabian Nights*, as though to block out reality. Another wad of bread hit him a few minutes later, and this time the laborers laughed. Dahlmann told himself he wasn't scared, but that it would be madness for him, a sick man, to be dragged by strangers into some chaotic bar fight. He made up his mind to leave; he was already on his feet when the storekeeper came over and urged him, his voice alarmed: "Sr. Dahlmann, ignore those boys over there—they're just feeling their oats."

Dahlmann did not find it strange that the storekeeper should know his name by now but he sensed that the man's conciliatory words actually made the situation worse. Before, the men's provocation had been directed at an accidental face, almost at nobody; now it was aimed at him, at his name, and the men at the other table would know that name. Dahlmann brushed the storekeeper aside, faced the laborers, and asked them what their problem was.

The young thug with the Indian-looking face stood up, stumbling as he did so. At one pace from Dahlmann, he shouted insults at him, as though he were far away. He was playacting, exaggerating his drunkenness, and the exaggeration produced an impression both fierce and mocking. Amid curses and obscenities, the man threw a long knife into the air, followed it with his eyes, caught it, and challenged Dahlmann to fight. The storekeeper's voice shook as he objected that Dahlmann was unarmed. At that point, something unforeseeable happened.

From out of a corner, the motionless old gaucho in whom Dahlmann had seen a symbol of the South (the South that belonged to him) tossed him a naked dagger—it came to rest at Dahlmann's feet. It was as though the South itself had decided that Dahlmann should accept the challenge. Dahlmann bent to pick up the dagger, and as he did he sensed two things: first, that that virtually instinctive action committed him to fight, and second, that in his clumsy hand the weapon would serve less to defend him than to justify the other man's killing him. He had toyed with a knife now and then, as all men did, but his knowledge of knife fighting went no further than a vague recollection that thrusts should be aimed upward, and with the blade facing inward. *They'd never have allowed this sort of thing to happen in the sanatorium,* he thought.

"Enough stalling," the other man said. "Let's go outside."

They went outside, and while there was no hope in Dahlmann, there was no fear, either. As he crossed the threshold, he felt that on that first night in the sanatorium, when they'd stuck that needle in him, dying in a knife fight under the open sky, grappling with his adversary, would have been a liberation, a joy, and a fiesta. He sensed that had he been able to choose or dream his death that night, this is the death he would have dreamed or chosen.

Dahlmann firmly grips the knife, which he may have no idea how to manage, and steps out into the plains.

Afterword by Andrew Hurley

In the late 1930s and early 1940s, Jorge Luis Borges was so productive that it is hard to imagine how one man did it all. In fact, over the course of those eight or nine years there seems never to have been a moment when he was not hard at work—writing introductions to friends' and acquaintances' books; translating Kafka, Virginia Woolf, and André Gide, among others; writing essays for other people's anthologies; compiling anthologies himself; going often to the movies and writing movie reviews; regularly contributing to, and on the editorial board of, the prestigious literary magazine *Sur*; and, for a popular magazine titled *El Hogar* ("Home"), writing dozens of literary and cultural columns and scores of book reviews of works in English, French, and German, in addition to Spanish.

But the truly amazing thing about Borges' work during these years is that in addition to his output in *belles-lettres* he was slowly and methodically producing one of the most influential collections of fiction in the twentieth century, a total of some seventeen stories that it is no exaggeration to say has changed the course of Western literature.

The first of these stories, "Pierre Menard, Author of the *Quixote*," appeared in May of 1939 in *Sur*.[1] A year later came "Tlön,

1. For the precise publishing information contained here, I wish most gratefully to acknowledge the important bibliographical work done by Nicolás Helft and published in *Jorge Luis Borges: Bibliografía completa* (Mexico City/Buenos Aires: Fondo de Cultura Económica, 1997).

Uqbar, Orbis Tertius," and six months after that, in December, 1940, "The Circular Ruins." Those three stories alone might have made any writer's reputation, but the next year saw more: "The Lottery in Babylon" and "An Examination of the Works of Herbert Quain"—this was January and April—and, on December 31 (the copyright actually says 1942), a volume entitled *The Garden of Forking Paths* that gathered together the stories just named above, picked up one ("The Approach to Al-Mu'tasim") that had been posing as a book review in a 1936 volume of essays, and added two theretofore unpublished stories: "The Library of Babel" and "The Garden of Forking Paths," which gave the volume its name.

Just under three years later, in 1944, Borges reprinted this collection, adding to it six stories that had been appearing one by one in *Sur* during the intervening months: "Death and the Compass" (May, 1942); "Funes, His Memory" (June); "The Shape of the Sword" (July); "The Secret Miracle" (February 1943); "The Theme of the Traitor and the Hero" (February, 1944); and "Three Versions of Judas" (August, 1944). These six new stories were gathered into their own section of the book and titled *Artifices*; they were also given their own introduction. (The first section retained the title *The Garden of Forking Paths*.) Because the volume itself had grown and changed so, it was given a new overall title, *Fictions*, and it was this volume, under that unassuming, almost generic title, that became one of the most celebrated "overnight successes" in twentieth-century literature.

Within a couple of years of this 1944 publication, translations of Borges' stories began appearing in France, first in a magazine called *Lettres Françaises* and then in a volume published in 1951 by Gallimard. And with the French appreciation of Borges came, in the course of things, translation into other languages, hundreds of thousands of readers, and the enormous influence that Borges exerts today on fiction in the West.

In 1956, after the French translations had been published and a select yet surprisingly wide audience throughout Europe, Britain, and the United States had begun to read and canonize Borges' work, he added three stories to *Fictions*. These, like so many of Borges' other stories, had first appeared in magazines; they were "The End" (October 1953), "The South" (February 1953), and "The Cult of the Phoenix" (September/October 1952). It may be their relative lateness that explains why these stories, though now an inseparable part of the volume, do not perhaps share the same degree of canonicity, are not perhaps so universally admired, as the earlier stories. For there is no question that it is those first stories (and especially "Pierre Menard," "Tlön," and "The Circular Ruins") that have become classics in modern and contemporary literature. As a group they are among the most read, commented-on, and alluded-to fictions of the century; indeed, despite the quality of so much of Borges' subsequent work, there are more than a few critics who contend that he never again reached the heights of achievement that he attained in these three stories.

Like most overnight successes, this one was a long time coming. It came, after all, when Borges was in his mid-forties and, despite his lack of fame, clearly an experienced writer. After all, he had been practicing his craft, *perfecting* his craft, for upwards of four decades: born in 1899, Borges had begun writing very precociously, when he was nine or ten years old. By his twentieth birthday he was deeply involved in his generation's "culture wars" on behalf of modern poetry in Europe. He was living comfortably with his family in Spain; he read constantly, everything he could get his hands on—good, bad, and mediocre—in four languages (French, German, English, and Spanish); and he had recently joined a group of young poets that called themselves the Ultraists. (He himself produced several of the manifestos that defined the movement.) By the time he was thirty, Borges had gone on to publish three volumes of poetry and three volumes of essays, and yet it was not until the age of thirty-five, relatively late in life in comparison with most writers, that he published his first volume of fiction, an eccentric collection of "creative biography" modeled a bit on Marcel Schwob's *Vies imaginaires*. But although *A Universal History of Iniquity* was a first volume, it was no mere apprentice-work, but rather a fully realized and unerringly executed volume.

Thus, by the time *Fictions* appeared, Borges had been consciously laboring at his craft for at least twenty-five years. His friends had recognized his remarkable talent all along; now it was the world's turn.

What was so new and striking about *Fictions* that wherever and whenever it appeared (because it did not appear in English until 1962) it immediately captured the imagination of readers? One thing was the prose itself. After a false start in his twenties with a highly baroque style employing strained and startling metaphors and a syntax that he later deplored as "writing Latin in Spanish," Borges had managed to craft a much quieter, subtler surface for his prose, and in fact by 1944 had become so adept at his terse and laconic Spanish style that readers and writers were beginning to call that particular style "Borgesian."

It was not style alone, though, that made such a stir among readers and writers. The stories themselves were unlike anything that readers had ever quite seen before. What was perhaps most immediately striking about them was their unclassifiability in terms of genre. Several of them—"Tlön, Uqbar, Orbis Tertius," "The Library of Babel," "The Lottery in Babylon," "The Circular Ruins," "The Secret Miracle," "The South"—seemed to belong to the genre of science fiction or fantasy, although in their treatment of their major themes (chance versus self-determination, the conception and writing of our history, the ideation and transmission of philosophical and mathematical systems, the existence of various levels and types of "reality," the immediacy and "reality" of the imagination) they were more erudite, more "philosophical," more "literate" than readers were accustomed to finding in such genre-stories. Four of the stories—"The Approach to Al-Mu'tasim," "Pierre Menard, Author of the *Quixote*," "A Survey of the Works of Herbert Quain," and "Three Versions of Judas"—looked like book reviews or critical monographs, albeit eccentric ones; so convincing was Borges' "note on an imaginary book" in the case of "The Approach to Al-Mu'tasim" that, when the story came out in 1935, Borges' close friend and sometime collaborator Adolfo Bioy Casares sent off for the apocryphal book from the putative publisher, Victor Gollancz, in England. Several of the stories started off by pretending to be reports of true incidents, either experienced by Borges himself, told him by an acquaintance, or taken from a discovered document, but then they spun off into what was clearly imaginative fiction; among these are "Funes, His Memory," "The Garden of Forking Paths," and "The Shape of the Sword." These fictions-about-fictions anticipated the metafictional concerns of postmodernism by decades, and they won Borges readers not only in the sixties, when they first appeared in English, but in more recent years as well, as English and American literature has become ever more concerned with the blurring lines between the Real and the Constructed, or between What Happened and How What-Happened Is Told. At least three of the stories in the volume—"The Garden of Forking Paths," "Death and the Compass," and "The Theme of the Traitor and the Hero"—borrowed heavily from detective fiction or murder-mysteries for their voice and their construction (not their plots *per se* but rather the author's plotting of the *narrative*, the subtle way that words and "facts" are used). Three of the stories—"The Circular Ruins," "The Lottery in Babylon," "The Cult of the Phoenix"—were told in a style that recalled myth, and were set in distant times and places that made them seem parables, both ageless and perfectly contemporary. (Note that some of the stories' titles appear two or three times in this catalog: further testimony to their unclassifiability.)

This playing with the boundaries of genre was echoed by a playfulness in both prose style and "attitude." Clearly, Borges was having fun with these stories. One could often catch him at his sport, as when he included the names of friends and enemies among the characters of the tales, for example, or made his narrator slightly mad and then called him "Borges." But there were times that even when readers saw something ludic in a story, they didn't always get the joke. Why, for example, in "The Lottery in Babylon," does Borges mention a "sacred latrine called Qaphqa [Kafka]"? Why in "The Library of Babel" does one of the indecipherable texts read *axaxaxas mlö*—why, when the *x*'s are pronounced with Spanish pronunciation, does one hear "a-hah-hah-hah mlu-u-uh," the author laughing and sticking out his tongue? Sometimes, one just had to sit back and enjoy *spotting* the playfulness; one learned that Borges' ways were mysterious and sometimes incomprehensible to men. And this ludic attitude existed even in the most serious of the stories, so that readers unaccustomed to such techniques were constantly being made to feel just a bit off balance. Was this serious, "high" literature that sometimes went just over one's head or was this sport, spoof, playing? The answer, almost all critics agreed, was both. And that, too, marked a new moment for literature in the twentieth century, for it reintroduced an overarching irony, a knowing worldliness (shared between the author and the reader) that had been driven underground by the high seriousness of the nineteenth century. For many readers, Borges recalled the wonderfully conspiratorial fictions of Sterne and Cervantes. Joyce, perhaps, had shared this attitude, but it had taken Joyce hundreds of pages and the invention of a new language to embody it; Borges could manage to convey it in three or four pages and in crystalline prose. What Borges gave the twentieth century, finally, was the whole tradition of Western (and some Eastern) literature and culture, under the aegis of *Als Ob*—Borges gave the century a license to *enjoy* its heritage, and to reinvent it for a new age.

The density of that heritage on any given page of Borges made readers realize how erudite the stories were, what an enormous range of writers, philosophers, historians, theologians, and other luminaries the stories referred or alluded to. Yet while the stories seemed remarkably "intellectual" and therefore somewhat forbidding, they were, at the same time, so hypnotic and so seductive and, with their judicious use of what Borges called "circumstantial details," so convincing, that readers found themselves more-than-willingly slipping into the literary games that the stories invited them to play.

It is perhaps this uncommon mix of erudition, philosophical seriousness, "literariness," and delighted, delightful fun that most distinguishes the fictions of Jorge Luis Borges, and that also makes them so inexhaustibly readable. Certainly *Fictions* offers all these readerly delights; perhaps, indeed, no collection of one author's short stories offers so many acknowledged masterpieces of the short story as this single volume does. It is Borges at the peak of his mature powers, the best of one of the century's greatest writers.

Andrew Hurley
San Juan, Puerto Rico
January 2000

A Note on the Translation

(from *Collected Fictions*)

The first known English translation of a work of fiction by the Argentine Jorge Luis Borges appeared in the August 1948 issue of *Ellery Queen's Mystery Magazine*, but although seven or eight more translations appeared in "little magazines" and anthologies during the fifties, and although Borges clearly had his champions in the literary establishment, it was not until 1962, fourteen years after that first appearance, that a book-length collection of fiction appeared in English.

The two volumes of stories that appeared in that *annus mirabilis*—one from Grove Press, edited by Anthony Kerrigan, and the other from New Directions, edited by Donald A. Yates and James E. Irby—caused an impact that was immediate and overwhelming. John Updike, John Barth, Anthony Burgess, and countless other writers and critics have eloquently and emphatically attested to the unsettling yet liberating effect that Jorge Luis Borges' work had on their vision of the way literature was thenceforth to be done. Reading those stories, writers and critics encountered a disturbingly *other* writer (Borges seemed, sometimes, to come from a place even more distant than Argentina, another literary planet), transported into their ken by translations, who took the detective story and turned it into metaphysics, who took fantasy writing and made it, with its questioning and reinventing of everyday reality, central to the craft of fiction. Even as early as 1933, Pierre Drieu La Rochelle, editor of the influential *Nouvelle Revue Française*, returning to France after visiting

Argentina, is famously reported to have said, *"Borges vaut le voyage";* now, thirty years later, readers didn't have to make the long, hard (though deliciously exotic) journey into Spanish—Borges had been brought to them, and indeed he soon was being paraded through England and the United States like one of those New World indigenes taken back, captives, by Columbus or Sir Walter Raleigh, to captivate the Old World's imagination.

But while for many readers of these translations Borges was a new writer appearing as though out of nowhere, the truth was that by the time we were reading Borges for the first time in English, he had been writing for forty years or more, long enough to have become a self-conscious, self-possessed, and self-*critical* master of the craft.

The reader of the forewords to the fictions will note that Borges is forever commenting on the style of the stories or the entire volume, preparing the reader for what is to come stylistically as well as thematically. More than once he draws our attention to the "plain style" of the pieces, in contrast to his earlier "baroque". And he is right: Borges' prose style is characterized by a determined economy of resources in which every word is weighted, every word (every mark of punctuation) "tells." It is a quiet style, whose effects are achieved not with bombast or pomp, but rather with a single exploding word or phrase, dropped almost as though offhandedly into a quiet sentence: "He examined his wounds and saw, without astonishment, that they had healed." This laconic detail ("without astonishment"), coming at the very beginning of "The Circular Ruins," will probably only at the end of the story be recalled by the reader, who will, retrospectively and somewhat abashedly, see that it changes *everything* in the story; it is quintessential Borges.

Quietness, subtlety, a laconic terseness—these are the marks of Borges' style. It is a style that has often been called intellectual, and indeed it is dense with allusion—to literature, to philosophy, to religion or theology, to myth, to the culture and history of

Buenos Aires and Argentina and the Southern Cone of South America, to the other contexts in which his words may have appeared. But it is also a simple style: Borges' sentences are almost invariably classical in their symmetry, in their balance. Borges likes parallelism, chiasmus, subtle repetitions-with-variations; his only indulgence in "shocking" the reader (an effect he repudiated) may be the "Miltonian displacement of adjectives" to which he alludes in his foreword to *The Maker*.

Another clear mark of Borges' prose is its employment of certain words with, or for, their etymological value. Again, this is an adjectival device, and it is perhaps the technique that is most unsettling to the reader. One of the most famous opening lines in Spanish literature is this: *Nadie lo vio desembarcar en la unánime noche*: "No one saw him slip from the boat in the unanimous night." What an odd adjective, "unanimous." It is so odd, in fact, that other translations have not allowed it. But it is just as odd in Spanish, and it clearly responds to Borges' intention, explicitly expressed in such fictions as "The Immortal," to let the Latin root govern the Spanish (and, by extension, English) usage. There is, for instance, a "splendid" woman: Her red hair glows. If the translator strives for similarity of effect in the translation (as I have), then he or she cannot, I think, avoid using this technique— which is a technique that Borges' beloved Emerson and de Quincey and Sir Thomas Browne also used with great virtuosity.

Borges himself was a translator of some note, and in addition to the translations per se that he left to Spanish culture—a number of German lyrics, Faulkner, Woolf, Whitman, Melville, Carlyle, Swedenborg, and others—he left at least three essays on the act of translation itself. Two of these, I have found, are extraordinarily liberating to the translator. In "Versions of Homer" ("Las versiones homéricas," 1932), Borges makes it unmistakably clear that every translation is a "version"—not *the* translation of Homer (or any other author) but *a* translation, one in a never-ending series, at least an infinite *possible* series. The very idea of *the* (definitive) translation is misguided, Borges tells us; there are only drafts, approximations—*versions*, as he insists on calling them. He chides us: "The concept of 'definitive text' is appealed to only by religion, or by weariness." Borges makes the point even more emphatically in his later essay "The Translators of the 1001 Nights" ("Los traductores de las *1001 Noches*," 1935).

If my count is correct, at least seventeen translators have preceded me in translating one or more of the fictions of Jorge Luis Borges. In most translator's notes, the translator would feel obliged to justify his or her new translation of a classic, to tell the potential reader of this new *version* that the shortcomings and errors of those seventeen or so prior translations have been met and conquered, as though they were enemies. Borges has tried in his essays to teach us, however, that we should not translate "against" our predecessors; a new translation is always justified by the new voice given the old work, by the new life in a new land that the translation confers on it, by the "shock of the new" that both old and new readers will experience from this inevitably new (or renewed) work. What Borges teaches is that we should simply commend the translation to the reader, with the hope that the reader will find in it a literary experience that is rich and moving. I have listened to Borges' advice as I have listened to Borges' fictions, and I—like the translators who have preceded me—have rendered Borges in the style that I hear when I listen to him. I think that the reader of my version will hear something of the genius of his storytelling and his style. For those who wish to read Borges as Borges wrote Borges, there is always *le voyage à l'espagnol*.

The text that the Borges estate specified to be used for this new translation is the three-volume *Obras completas*, published by Emecé Editores in 1989.

In producing this translation, it has not been our intention to produce an annotated or scholarly edition of Borges, but rather a "reader's edition." Thus, bibliographical information (which is often confused or terribly complex even in the most reliable of cases) has not been included except in a couple of clear instances, nor have we taken variants into account in any way; the Borges Foundation is reported to be working on a fully annotated, bibliographically reasoned variorum, and scholars of course can go to the several bibliographies and many other references that now exist. I have, however, tried to provide the Anglophone reader with at least a modicum of the general knowledge of the history, literature, and culture of Argentina and the Southern Cone of South America that a Hispanophone reader of the fictions, growing up in that culture, would inevitably have. To that end, asterisks have been inserted into the text of the fictions, tied to corresponding notes at the back of the book. (The notes often cite sources where interested readers can find further information.)

One particularly thorny translation decision that had to be made involved *A Universal History of Iniquity*. This volume is purportedly a series of biographies of reprehensible evildoers, and as biography, the book might be expected to rely greatly upon "sources" of one sort or another—as indeed Borges' "Index of Sources" seems to imply. In his preface to the 1954 reprinting of the volume, however, Borges acknowledges the "fictive" nature of his stories: This is a case, he says, of "changing and distorting (sometimes without æsthetic justification) the stories of other men" to produce a work singularly his own. This sui generis use of sources, most of which were in English, presents the translator with something of a challenge: to translate Borges even while Borges is cribbing from, translating, and "changing and distorting" other writers' stories. The method I have chosen to employ is to go to the sources Borges names, to see the ground upon which those changes and distortions were wrought; where Borges is clearly translating phrases, sentences, or even larger pieces of text, I have used the English of the original source. Thus, the New York gangsters in "Monk Eastman" speak as Asbury quotes them, not as I might have translated Borges' Spanish into English had I been translating in the usual sense of the word; back-translating Borges' translation did not seem to make much sense. But even while returning to the sources, I have made no attempt, either in the text or in my notes, to "correct" Borges; he has changed names (or their spellings), dates, numbers, locations, etc., as his literary vision led him to, but the tracing of those "deviations" is a matter which the editors and I have decided should be left to critics and scholarly publications.

More often than one would imagine, Borges' characters are murderers, knife fighters, throat slitters, liars, evil or casually violent men and women—and of course many of them "live" in a time different from our own. They sometimes use language that is strong, and that today may well be offensive—words denoting membership in ethnic and racial groups, for example. In the Hispanic culture, however, some of these expressions can be, and often are, used as terms of endearment—*negro/negra* and *chino/china* come at once to mind. (I am not claiming that Argentina is free of bigotry; Borges chronicles that, too.) All this is to explain a decision as to my translation of certain terms—specifically *rusito* (literally "little Russian," but with the force of "Jew," "sheeny"), *pardo/parda* (literally "dark mulatto," "black-skinned"), and *gringo* (meaning Italian immigrants: "wops," etc.)—that Borges uses in his fictions. I have chosen to use the word "sheeny" for *rusito* and the word "wop" for *gringo* because in the stories in which these words appear, there is an intention to be offensive—a *character's* intention, not Borges'. I have also chosen to use the word "nigger" for *pardo/parda*. This decision is taken not without considerable soul-searching, but I feel there is historical justification for it. In the May 20, 1996, edition of *The New Yorker* magazine, p. 63, the respected historian and cultural critic Jonathan Raban noted the existence of a nineteenth-century "Nigger Bob's saloon," where, out on the Western frontier, husbands would await the arrival of the train bringing their wives from the East. Thus, when a character in one of Borges' stories says, "I knew I could count on you, old nigger," one can almost hear the slight tenderness, or respect, in the voice, even if, at the same time, one winces. In my view, it is not the translator's place to (as Borges put it) "soften or mitigate" these words. Therefore, I have translated the epithets with the words I believe would have been used in English—in the United States, say—at the time the stories take place.

The footnotes that appear throughout the text of the stories in the *Collected Fictions* are Borges' own, even when they say "Ed."

This translation commemorates the centenary of Borges' birth in 1899; I wish it also to mark the fiftieth anniversary of the first appearance of Borges in English, in 1948. It is to all translators, then, Borges included, that this translation is—unanimously—dedicated.

Andrew Hurley
San Juan, Puerto Rico
June 1998

Acknowledgments

(from *Collected Fictions*)

I am indebted to the University of Puerto Rico at Río Piedras for a sabbatical leave that enabled me to begin this project. My thanks to the administration, and to the College of Humanities and the Department of English, for their constant support of my work not only on this project but throughout my twenty-odd years at UPR.

The University of Texas at Austin, Department of Spanish and Portuguese, and its director, Madeline Sutherland-Maier, were most gracious in welcoming the stranger among them. The department sponsored me as a Visiting Scholar with access to all the libraries at UT during my three years in Austin, where most of this translation was produced. My sincerest gratitude is also owed those libraries and their staffs, especially the Perry-Castañeda, the Benson Latin American Collection, and the Humanities Research Center (HRC). Most of the staff, I must abashedly confess, were nameless to me, but one person, Cathy Henderson, has been especially important, as the manuscripts for this project have been incorporated into the Translator Archives in the HRC.

For many reasons this project has been more than usually complex. At Viking Penguin, my editors, Kathryn Court and Michael Millman, have been steadfast, stalwart, and (probably more often than they would have liked) inspired in seeing it through. One could not possibly have had more supportive colleagues, or co-conspirators who stuck by one with any greater solidarity.

Many, many people have given me advice, answered questions, and offered support of all kinds—they know who they are, and will forgive me, I know, for not mentioning them all personally; I have been asked to keep these acknowledgments brief. But two people, Carter Wheelock and Margaret Sayers Peden, have contributed in an especially important and intimate way, and my gratitude to them cannot go unexpressed here. Carter Wheelock read word by word through an "early-final" draft of the translation, comparing it against the Spanish for omissions, misperceptions and mistranslations, and errors of fact. This translation is the cleaner and more honest for his efforts. Margaret Sayers Peden (a.k.a. Petch), one of the finest translators from Spanish working in the world today, was engaged by the publisher to be an outside editor for this volume. Petch read through the late stages of the translation, comparing it with the Spanish, suggesting changes that ranged from punctuation to "readings." Translators want to translate, *love* to translate; for a translator at the height of her powers to read a translation in this painstaking way and yet, while suggesting changes and improvements, to respect the other translator's work, his approach, his thought processes and creativity—even to applaud the other translator's (very) occasional strokes of brilliance—is to engage in an act of selflessness that is almost superhuman. She made the usual somewhat tedious editing process a joy.

I would never invoke Carter Wheelock's and Petch Peden's readings of the manuscripts of this translation—or those of Michael Millman and the other readers at Viking Penguin—as giving it any authority or credentials or infallibility beyond its fair deserts, but I must say that those readings have given me a security in this translation that I almost surely would not have felt so strongly without them. I am deeply and humbly indebted.

First, last, always, and in number of words inversely proportional to my gratitude—I thank my wife, Isabel Garayta.

Andrew Hurley
San Juan, Puerto Rico
June 1998

Notes to the Fictions

(from *Collected Fictions*)

These notes are intended only to supply information that a Latin American (and especially Argentine or Uruguayan) reader would have and that would color or determine his or her reading of the stories. Generally, therefore, the notes cover only Argentine history and culture; I have presumed the reader to possess more or less the range of general or world history or culture that JLB makes constant reference to, or to have access to such reference books and other sources as would supply any need there. There is no intention here to produce an "annotated Borges," but rather only to illuminate certain passages that might remain obscure, or even be misunderstood, without that information.

For these notes, I am deeply indebted to *A Dictionary of Borges* by Evelyn Fishburn and Psiche Hughes (London: Duckworth, 1990). Other dictionaries, encyclopedias, reference books, biographies, and works of criticism have been consulted, but none has been as thorough and immediately useful as the *Dictionary of Borges*. In many places, and especially where I quote Fishburn and Hughes directly, I cite their contribution, but I have often paraphrased them without direct attribution; I would not want anyone to think, however, that I am unaware or unappreciative of the use I have made of them. Any errors are my own responsibility, of course, and should not be taken to reflect on them or their work in any way. Another book that has been invaluable is Emir Rodríguez Monegal's *Jorge Luis Borges: A Literary Biography* (New York: Paragon Press, [paper] 1988), now out of print. In the notes, I have cited this work as "Rodríguez Monegal, p. x."

The names of Arab and Persian figures that appear in the stories are taken, in the case of historical persons, from the English transliterations of Philip K. Hitti in his work *History of the Arabs from the Earliest Times to the Present* (New York: Macmillan, 1951). (JLB himself cites Hitti as an authority in this field.) In the case of fictional characters, the translator has used the system of transliteration implicit in Hitti's historical names in comparison with the same names in Spanish transliteration—*Translator*.

Fictions

p. 1: Title. First published as *Ficciones* (1935–1944) by Editorial Sur in 1944, this book was made up of two volumes: *El jardín de senderos que se bifurcan* ("The Garden of Forking Paths"), which had originally been published in 1941–1942, and *Artificios* ("Artifices"), dated 1944 and never before published as a book. Each volume in the 1944 edition had its own title page and its own preface. (In that edition, and in all successive editions, *The Garden of Forking Paths* included the story "El acercamiento a Al-motasím" ("The Approach to Al-Mu'tasim"), collected first in *Historia de la eternidad* ("History of Eternity"), 1936, and reprinted in each successive edition of that volume until 1953; this story now appears in the *Obras Completas* in *Historia de la eternidad*, but it is included here as a "fiction" rather than an "essay.") In 1956 Emecé published a volume titled *Ficciones*, which was identical to the 1944 Editorial Sur edition except for the inclusion in *Artificios* of three new stories ("The End," "The Cult of the Phoenix," and "The South") and a "Postscript" to the 1944 preface to *Artificios*. It is this 1956 edition of *Fictions*, plus "The Approach to Al-Mu'tasim," that is translated for this book.

The Garden of Forking Paths

Foreword

p. 5: The eight stories: The eighth story, here printed as the second, "The Approach to Al-Mu'tasim," was included in all editions subsequent to the 1941–1942 original edition. It had originally been published (1936) in *Historia de la eternidad* ("A History of Eternity"). Ordinals and cardinals used in the Foreword have been adjusted to reflect the presence of this story.

p. 5: Sur: "[T]he most influential literary publication in Latin

America" (Rodríguez Monegal, p. 233), it was started by Victoria Ocampo, with the aid of the Argentine novelist Eduardo Mallea and the American novelist Waldo Frank. Borges was one of the journal's first contributors, certainly one of its most notable (though *Sur* published or discussed virtually every major poet, writer, and essayist of the New or Old World) and he acted for three decades as one of its "guardian angels." Many of JLB's fictions, some of his poetry, and many critical essays and reviews appeared for the first time in the pages of *Sur*.

Tlön, Uqbar, Orbis Tertius

p. 7: Ramos Mejía: "A part of Buenos Aires in which the rich had weekend houses containing an English colony. It is now an industrial suburb" (Hughes and Fishburn).

p. 7: Bioy Casares: Adolfo Bioy Casares (1914–): Argentine novelist, JLB's closest friend and collaborator with JLB on numerous projects, including some signed with joint pseudonyms. In their joint productions, the two men were interested in detective stories, innovative narrative techniques (as the text here hints), and tales of a somewhat "fantastic" nature. Unfortunately rather eclipsed by Borges, especially in the English-speaking world, Bioy Casares is a major literary figure with a distinguished body of work; a description of the reciprocal influence of the two writers would require (at least) its own book-length study.

p. 8: Volume XLVI: The *Obras completas,* on which this translation is based, has "Volume XXVI," which the translator takes to be a typographical error, the second X slipped in for the correct *L.*

p. 9: Johannes Valentinus Andreä in the writings of Thomas de Quincey: It is perhaps significant that de Quincey credits Andreä (1586–1654) with "inventing" the Rosicrucian order by writing satirical works (and one especially: *Fama Fraternitatis of the meritorious Order of the Rosy Cross, addressed to the learned in general and the Governors of Europe*) describing an absurd mystico-Christian secret society engaged not only in general beneficence and the improvement of humanity but also in alchemy and gold making. The public did not perceive Andreä's satirical intent, and many rushed to "join" this society, though they could never find anyone to admit them. At last, according to de Quincey, a group of "Paracelsists" decided that if nobody else would admit to being a Rosicrucian, *they* would take over the name and "be" the society.

p. 10: Carlos Mastronardi: Mastronardi (1901–1976) was "a poet, essayist, and journalist [in Buenos Aires], a member of the group of writers identified with the avant-garde literary magazine *Martín Fierro*" (Fishburn and Hughes). Balderston (*The Literary Universe of JLB*: An Index . . . [New York: Greenwood Press], 1986) gives some of his titles: *Luz de Provincia, Tierra amanecida, Conocimiento de la noche.* Mastronardi was one of JLB's closest friends throughout the thirties and forties (Borges too was closely associated with *Martín Fierro*), and Rodríguez Monegal reported in his biography of JLB that Borges was still seeing Mastronardi as the biography (publ. 1978) was written; it seems safe to say, therefore, that Borges and Mastronardi were friends until Mastronardi's death.

p. 11: Capangas: Overseers or foremen of gangs of workers, usually either slaves or indentured semislaves, in rural areas, for cutting timber, etc., though not on ranches, where the foreman is known as a *capataz.* This word is of Guaraní or perhaps African origin and came into Spanish, as JLB indicates, from the area of Brazil.

p. 12: Néstor Ibarra: (b. 1908) "Born in France of an Argentine father who was the son of a French Basque émigré, *NI* went to the University of Buenos Aires around 1925 to complete his graduate education. While [there] he discovered Borges' poems and . . . tried to persuade his teachers to let him write a thesis on Borges' ultraist poetry" (Rodríguez Monegal, p. 239). Ibarra's groundbreaking and very important study of JLB, *Borges et Borges*, and his translations of JLB (along with those of Roger Caillois) into French in the 1950s were instrumental in the worldwide recognition of JLB's greatness. Among the other telling associations with this and other stories is the fact that Ibarra and Borges invented a new language ("with surrealist or ultraist touches"), a new French school of literature, Identism, "in which objects were always compared to themselves," and a new review, titled *Papers for the Suppression of Reality* (see "Pierre Menard," in this volume; this information, Rodríguez Monegal, pp. 240–241). The *N.R.F.* is the *Nouvelle Revue Française*, an extremely important French literary magazine that published virtually every important modern writer in the first three decades of this century.

p. 12: Ezequiel Martínez Estrada: Martínez Estrada (1895–1964) was an influential Argentine writer whose work *Radiografía de la pampa*

(*X-ray of the Pampa*) JLB reviewed very favorably in 1933 in the literary supplement (*Revista Multicolor de los Sábados* ["Saturday Motley Review"]) to the Buenos Aires newspaper *Crítica*.

p. 12: Drieu La Rochelle: Pierre-Eugene Drieu La Rochelle (1893–1945) was for a time the editor of the *Nouvelle Revue Française*; he visited Argentina in 1933, recognized JLB's genius, and is reported to have said on his return to France that "*Borges vaut le voyage*" (Fishburn and Hughes).

p. 12: Alfonso Reyes: Reyes (1889–1959) was a Mexican poet and essayist, ambassador to Buenos Aires (1927–1930 and again 1936–1937), and friend of JLB's (Fishburn and Hughes). Reyes is recognized as one of the great humanists of the Americas in the twentieth century, an immensely cultured man who was a master of the Spanish language and its style ("direct and succinct without being thin or prosaic" [Rodríguez Monegal]).

p. 13: Xul Solar: Xul Solar is the nom de plume-turned-name of Alejandro Schultz (1887–1963), a lifelong friend of JLB; JLB compared Xul favorably with William Blake. Xul was a painter and something of a "creative linguist," having invented a language he called creol: a "language ... made up of Spanish enriched by neologisms and by monosyllabic English words ... used as adverbs" (Roberto Alifano, interviewer and editor, *Twenty-Four Conversations with Borges*, trans. Nicomedes Suárez Araúz, Willis Barnstone, and Noemí Escandell [Housatonic, Mass.: Lascaux Publishers, 1984], p. 119). In another place, JLB also notes another language invented by Xul Solar: "a philosophical language after the manner of John Wilkins" ("Autobiographical Essay," p. 237: *The Aleph and Other Stories: 1933–1969* [New York: Dutton, 1970], pp. 203–260). JLB goes on to note that "Xul was his version of Schultz and Solar of Solari." Xul Solar's painting has often been compared with that of Paul Klee; "strange" and "mysterious" are adjectives often applied to it. Xul illustrated three of JLB's books: *El tamaño de mi esperanza* (1926), *El idioma de los argentinos* (1928), and *Un modelo para la muerte*, the collaboration between JLB and Adolfo Bioy Casares that was signed "B. Suárez Lynch." In his biography of Borges, Emir Rodríguez Monegal devotes several pages to Xul's influence on JLB's writing; Borges himself also talks at length about Xul in the anthology of interviews noted above. Xul was, above all, a "character" in the Buenos Aires of the twenties and thirties and beyond.

p. 22: Amorim: Enrique Amorim (1900–1960) was a Uruguayan novelist, related to Borges by marriage. He wrote about the pampas, the gaucho, and gaucho life; Borges thought his *El Paisano Aguilar* "a closer description of gaucho life than Güiraldes' more famous *Don Segundo Sombra*" (Fishburn and Hughes).

Pierre Menard, Author of the Quixote

p. 40: Local color in Maurice Barrès or Rodríguez Larreta: Barrès (1862–1923) was a "French writer whose works include a text on bull-fighting entitled *Du sang, de la volupté et de la mort*" (Fishburn and Hughes); one can see what the narrator is getting at in terms of romanticizing the foreign. Enrique Rodríguez Larreta (1875–1961) wrote historical novels; one, set in Avila and Toledo in the time of Philip II (hence the reference to that name in the text) and titled *La gloria de Don Ramiro*, used an archaic Spanish for the dialogue; clearly this suggests the archaism of Menard's *Quixote*. (Here I paraphrase Fishburn and Hughes.)

A Survey of the Works of Herbert Quain

p. 60: The Siamese Twin Mystery: A novel by Ellery Queen, published in 1933. Here the literary critic–narrator is lamenting the fact that Quain's novel was overshadowed by the much more popular Queen's.

Artifices

Funes, His Memory

p. 91: Title: This story has generally appeared under the title "Funes the Memorious," and it must be the brave (or foolhardy) translator who dares change such an odd and memorable title. Nor would the translator note (and attempt to justify) his choice of a translation except in unusual circumstances. Here, however, the title in the original Spanish calls for some explanation. The title is "Funes el memorioso"; the word *memorioso* is not an odd Spanish word; it is in fact perfectly common, if somewhat colloquial. It simply means "having a wonderful or powerful memory," what in English one might render by the expression "having a memory like an elephant." The beauty of the Spanish is that the entire long phrase is compressed into a single word, a single adjective, used in the original title as an epithet: Funes the Elephant-Memoried. (The reader can see that that translation won't do.) The word "memorist" is perhaps the closest thing that common English yields up without inventing a new word such as "memorious," which strikes the current translator as vaguely Lewis Carroll-esque, yet "memorist" has something vaguely show business about it, as though Funes worked vaudeville or the carnival sideshows. The French title of this story is the lovely eighteenth-century-sounding *"Funes ou La Mémoire"*; with a nod to JLB's great admirer John Barth, I have chosen "Funes, His Memory."

p. 91: The Banda Oriental: The "eastern bank" of the River Plate, the old name of Uruguay before it became a country, and a name used for many years afterward by the "old-timers" or as a sort of nickname.

p. 91: Pedro Leandro Ipuche: The Uruguayan Ipuche was a friend of the young ultraist-period Borges (ca. 1925), with whom (along with Ricardo Güiraldes, author of the important novel *Don Segundo Sombra*) he worked on the literary magazine *Proa* (Fishburn and Hughes). *Proa* was an influential little magazine, and Borges and friends took it seriously; they were engaged, as Rodríguez Monegal quotes the "Autobiographical Essay" as saying, in "renewing both prose and poetry."

p. 92: Fray Bentos: "A small town on the banks of the Uruguay River, famous for its meat-canning industry. In his youth Borges was a regular visitor to his cousins' ranch near Fray Bentos" (Fishburn and Hughes). Haedo was in fact the family name of these cousins.

p. 97: The thirty-three Uruguayan patriots: The "Thirty-three," as they were called, were a band of determined patriots under the leadership of Juan Antonio Lavalleja who crossed the River Plate from Buenos Aires to Montevideo in order to "liberate" the Banda Oriental (Uruguay) from the Spaniards. Their feat of bravery, under impossible odds, immortalized them in the mythology of the Southern Cone. For fuller detail, see the note to p. 474, for the story "Avelino Arredondo" in the volume *The Book of Sand*.

Three Versions of Judas

p. 135 (note): *Euclides da Cunha:* Cunha (1866–1909) was a very well-known Brazilian writer whose most famous novel is a fictional retelling of an uprising in the state of Bahía. He was moved by the spiritualism (Fishburn and Hughes note its mystical qualities) of the rebels.

p. 135 (note): *Antonio Conselheiro:* (1828–1897). Conselheiro was "a Brazilian religious dissident who led a rebellion in Canudos, in the northern state of Bahía. The rebels were peasants ... who lived in a system of communes, working out their own salvation. They rose against the changes introduced by the new Republican government, which they regarded as the Antichrist. ...Conselheiro's head was cut off and put on public display" (Fishburn and Hughes). His real name was Antonio Maciel; *conselheiro* means "counselor," and so his messianic, ministerial role is here emphasized.

p. 135 (note): *Almafuerte:* The pseudonym of Pedro Bonifacio Palacio (1854–1917), one of Argentina's most beloved poets. A kind of role model and hero to young writers, akin to the phenomenon of Dylan Thomas in Britain and the United States a few years ago, Almafuerte was one of JLB's most admired contemporaries.

The End

p. 139: "It'd been longer than seven years that I'd gone without seeing my children. I found them that day, and I wouldn't have it so's I looked to them like a man on his way to a knife fight": It is not these words that need noting, but an "intertextual event." It is about here that the Argentine reader will probably realize what this story is about: It is a retelling of the end of José Hernández' famous tale *Martín Fierro*. As Fierro is a knife fighter, and as a black man figures in the poem, and as there is a famous song contest, the reader will put two and two together, no doubt, even before Martín Fierro's name is mentioned a few lines farther on. This is the way Fishburn and Hughes state the situation: "The episode alluded to in 'The End' is the *payada*, or song contest, between Martín Fierro and *el moreno* ["the black man"] who was the brother of the murdered negro. In the contest the gauchos discuss metaphysical themes, but towards the end *el moreno* reveals his identity, and his desire for revenge is made clear. In keeping with the more conciliatory tone of pt. 2 [of Hernández' original poem] a fight is prevented between the two contestants, each going his own way. 'The End' is a gloss on this episode, the fight that might have taken place." By this late in the volume, JLB's Preface to the stories, hinting at the coexistence of a "famous book" in this story, may have dimmed in the reader's memory, but for the Latin American reader, the creeping familiarity of the events, like the echoes of Shakespeare in the assassination of Kilpatrick in "Theme of the Traitor and the Hero," should come into the foreground in this section of the story, and the reader, like Ryan in that other story, make the "connection."

The South

p. 146: Buenos Aires: Here the province, not the city. The reference is to the northern border, near Entre Ríos and Santa Fe provinces, on the Paraná River.

p. 146: Catriel: Cipriano Catriel (d. 1874). Catriel was an Indian chieftain who fought against the Argentines in the Indian wars. Later, however, he fought on the side of the revolutionary forces (Fishburn and Hughes).

p. 151: His gaucho trousers: This is the *chiripá*, a triangular worsted shawl tied about the waist with the third point pulled up between the legs and looped into a knot to form a rudimentary pant, or a sort of diaper. It is worn over a pair of pantaloons (ordinarily white) that "stick out" underneath. Sometimes, incredible as it strikes Anglo-Saxons that the extraordinarily *machista* gauchos would wear such clothing (but think of the Scots' kilts), the pantaloons had lace bottoms.